SEEING RED

Skye Fargo could still recall the scene in the looted cabin. The woman who had been raped and killed. The two little boys who had been killed as well.

He could recall when he yanked the gunman named Clement away from the next victim of his twisted lust. Clement flew backward, landing sprawled on his behind.

"What the hell are you doing?" Clement demanded.

"What am I doing?" Fargo countered, and brought up his Colt. The unwritten rule was to shoot to kill or not to shoot at all. Fargo didn't have any problem making up his mind. He wanted to kill. His only question was which way would make it hurt the most. . . .

DEATH'S CARAVAN

by

Jon Sharpe

Ⓢ
A SIGNET BOOK

NEW AMERICAN LIBRARY

A DIVISION OF PENGUIN BOOKS USA INC.

PUBLISHER'S NOTE

This is a work of fiction. Names, characters, places, and incidents either are the product of the author's imagination or are used fictitiously, and any resemblance to actual persons, living or dead, events, or locales is entirely coincidental.

Copyright © 1989 by Jon Sharpe

The first chapter of this book previously appeared in *Cave of Death*, the ninety-first volume in this series.

First Printing, August, 1989

1 2 3 4 5 6 7 8 9

The Trailsman

Beginnings . . . they bend the tree and they mark the man. Skye Fargo was born when he was eighteen. Terror was his midwife, vengeance his first cry. Killing spawned Skye Fargo, ruthless, cold-blooded murder. Out of the acrid smoke of gunpowder still hanging in the air, he rose, cried out a promise never forgotten.

The Trailsman, they began to call him all across the West: searcher, scout, hunter, the man who could see where others only looked, his skills for hire but not his soul, the man who lived each day to the fullest, yet trailed each tomorrow. Skye Fargo, the Trailsman, the seeker who could take the wildness of a land and the wanting of a woman and make them his own.

*Summer, 1864. The Plains Indians have taken
to the warpath. The telegraph is cut,
no stages run, no wagon trains roll.
The Great Platte River Road is closed.
A fortune awaits the first man who can get
a caravan to Denver—if he can live
long enough to enjoy it . . .*

1

The stars pulsated like lightning bugs on a summer's eve while meteors spilled out of the Big Dipper and splashed onto the Milky Way, leaving colorful trails behind. Streaks of crimson, emerald, and violet exploded like Chinese fireworks on the Fourth of July, until someone stepped in the way.

Skye Fargo lay flat on his back. Some stranger stood at his feet. For a moment, Fargo was merely taken aback, since the intruder seemed to come from nowhere, rising like a mist to hover over him. But the stranger's shadow grew and loomed over the Trailsman, blotting out the stars beyond as it descended like a hawk swooping upon a rabbit.

Fargo instinctively rolled, but the surface beside him gave way and he fell several feet. His shoulder hit first, then his skull cracked against something hard. The blow made him dizzy, but there was no time to hesitate. Something loomed over him, something large and dark and ominous.

As he struggled to sit up, Fargo heard a sharp intake of breath; the sound was definitely human. Dazzling light assaulted the Trailsman as he opened his eyes, but he caught the flurry of movement before him. He launched himself at it. Unerringly, he grasped the intruder around the knees and brought him down. Hands flew at Fargo's face and thumped against his shoulders, but he subdued them quickly.

As Fargo struggled to gain his breath, the body pinned beneath his own ceased squirming.

"Sally?" Fargo murmured, staring at the woman in his arms.

Sally's eyes were wide with shock, and the sprinkle of freckles across her nose looked dark against her pale skin. She didn't answer. Instead, her chin trembled.

"What's going on?" he wondered, glancing across the plank floor. Feeling stunned, Fargo gazed at the dresser, then up at the gauze curtains, before looking back over his shoulder at the four-poster behind him. It must have been a dream, he thought, although he certainly couldn't remember ever having had one like it. He was positive he'd never come awake in quite this way before.

Of course it was a dream. Stars didn't flit around like fireflies. They didn't explode in vivid color. But Fargo couldn't shake the feeling of impending danger. He couldn't quite believe that the huge shadow hanging over him had been nothing more than Sally—sweet, plump Sally.

Studying her with his lake-blue eyes, Fargo gripped Sally's shoulders a bit too tightly. "Are you hurt?" he demanded. His voice grated with the aftermath of action.

Sally flinched away as if he had meant to strike her. Her eyelids squeezed shut. A tear trickled from beneath her long lashes.

The Trailsman realized his mistake instantly. He was still too keyed up. His body was rigid with tension. His fingers grasped like talons.

Waking up so abruptly had left him with a strange sense of unreality. His dreams still seemed more real than this woman and this room. Fargo scowled as the light pouring through the window assaulted his eyes and the blood pulsing in his temples drummed an annoying staccato.

His features were grim as he attempted to quell his pain. He felt cotton-mouthed and weary, but his high Cherokee cheekbones and darkly bearded jaw remained stern. Realizing that his visage must look absolutely thunderous, Fargo willed himself to relax.

He wanted to say something comforting to Sally, but the words were curiously remote; he couldn't seem to organize them enough to get them out.

Sally sniveled, but she didn't look hurt. She wasn't wincing or crying. She was merely scared. "Oh, Lord," she whispered. "What are you going to do to me?" Before he could respond, Sally choked on a stifled sob. "Oh, God, how did you find out?" she wailed. "I didn't mean anything by it. Really I didn't. I left you a whole thousand dollars in your saddlebags. I wasn't going to cheat you."

Astounded, Fargo stared at her as she turned her face back toward him. Her cheeks were splotched, her lashes wet, her eyes pleading. He had no idea what she was babbling about.

"Oh, Skye, you know I wouldn't hurt you, don't you?" Sally raised her hand to caress his cheek, but it was Fargo's turn to flinch. He drew back in suspicion.

"I was real careful. I didn't give you anything the girls don't take all the time. Just a little bit of laudanum, and some of that belladonna stuff Jolie uses. She says it keeps her cheeks flushed and her eyes sparkling. And some herbs."

"Herbs?" Fargo blurted.

"Herbs. Myra got them from one of those Chinese doctors in San Francisco. You know," Sally revealed nervously. "He has one of those little back-street opium dens. That's why Myra had to come back here. In Frisco she spent all her time in those places. Didn't make a lick of money. But the herbs are all right. I swear it. They just help her sleep some, that's all."

"How, Sally?" Fargo urged, wishing she would stay on the subject that concerned him. He didn't even know who Myra was, and he already felt confused enough.

Sally stared at Fargo blankly for a minute. Finally understanding his question, she lowered her damp lashes. Her body convulsed under his. "Please, Skye. Please don't be mad. I just put some in the whiskey. And some in that chew I gave you. Except then I got a little scared since you didn't like that chew much. And I put some in the coffee. But that's all. I swear that's all."

"That's all," Fargo repeated, gazing down at her in astonishment, his fingers still clamped on her shoulders.

"Please, Skye, you're not going to kill me, are you?" Sally moaned.

Laudanum and belladonna and herbs. God only knew what kind of herbs. No wonder his head was still spinning and those dreams had been so vivid. No wonder he was still too damn confused.

"And I did stay with you, didn't I?" she continued plaintively. "I didn't just leave you alone. I wasn't going to leave until you started stirring. But you didn't just stir," she reflected, bewilderment glistening in her eyes. "You just sprang right out like a wildcat. One minute you were down, and then you flew right off that bed and leapt on me like a panther. I'm not really sure what happened."

"That makes two of us," Fargo admitted, remembering his dream.

"I should have expected it, though," she prattled breathlessly. "After all, you are the Trailsman. And what I did, it won't make any difference," she assured him. "You can catch up with them any day. You're the best."

"Catch up with who?"

Sally was talking too much for him. That was her habit, but before now Fargo had felt no compulsion to watch her lips and listen to the chaotic tumult as if it were music, a peculiar music as shrill as bagpipes. She was terrified, he realized. It made her voice rise; it made her talk more than she usually did, which was already much more than enough.

"Why, with Webster and McCormick, of course," she spluttered. "Who else?"

"Webster and McCormick," Fargo repeated dully, and took a deep breath. He had to get a hold of himself, but his head felt much too heavy. Just thinking seemed to steam up his brain and fill his skull with dense fog.

"What do Webster and McCormick have to do with this?" he asked finally, his words succinct, his delivery almost melodious. Relief surged through him. He was all right. His thoughts began to jell.

"They're the ones that paid me," Sally answered. "You didn't think I did this all on my own, did you?"

Fargo didn't bother to answer. "What did they pay you for?" he asked instead.

"Why, to delay you, of course. What did you think?"

Fargo rolled off her and sat up. "Damn," he muttered, pressing his palms against his temples.

He realized he was naked. He might have felt a little foolish if his head hadn't been throbbing too much to allow for any other feelings. Fargo struggled to stand. He had to grab a bedpost as the room tilted sickeningly. The floor slowly righted itself.

"Oh, Skye," Sally blurted. "I'm sorry. Does your head hurt? Is it my fault?"

He swung toward her—a mistake, because the contents of his skull didn't turn nearly as quickly as his head. "Yes," he snapped.

Clinging to the bedpost, he stood for several seconds, waiting for his temper to kick in. But it all seemed too preposterous. Webster and McCormick were freighters, nothing more. For the last week Fargo had been trying to get them to combine trains with him, but they had insisted that he just didn't want them to pull into Denver first. As if it mattered.

The Great Platte River Road was nearly impassable because of an Indian uprising. Anyone getting anything to Denver would get premium rates. First or second didn't matter. Fargo's own shipment was already contracted at fifty cents per pound; the normal rate was ten cents.

"So how much damage is done?" he asked.

"What?" Sally whispered.

"What time is it?"

"Thursday. Noon or so."

13

"Are you trying to tell me I've been lying in that bed for three days?"

"Oh, no," she protested. "You were up lots. You just weren't real clear about things. Of course, I had to keep giving you more whiskey so you didn't come clear out of it, but we had lots and lots of fun." Sally sighed wistfully.

"Sorry I missed it," Fargo muttered.

"You're not going to kill me, are you, Skye?" Her voice cracked as it swept up in that anxious, too-high, falsetto she'd been plying him with since he'd woke up.

It made him feel almost sorry for her; except, if it wasn't for her, his brain wouldn't have been bucking against his skull like an ornery mule. "Don't ask me that," he barked. "Don't give me any ideas."

Sally gazed up with liquid brown eyes. Bright-pink tear splotches covered the freckles on her cheeks. Just looking at her made Fargo figure he should have known better.

He'd been around enough to know that women were seldom what they looked to be, and this one had the kind of butter-wouldn't-melt-in-her-mouth, apple-cheeked, country-milkmaid exterior that should have alerted him instantly. She sat cross-legged on the floor with her brightly colored robe billowing around her. Her hair was tied back in a blue velvet ribbon, but her head was tilted just right so that a few long brown curls spilled across her shoulder and down over her left breast. Fargo wondered if that was another of her sweet schoolgirl poses.

"Goddammit, what about Amos?" he blustered abruptly. "Where is he? Hasn't he been looking for me?"

"I told him you had some sudden unexpected business come up and wouldn't be leaving until Friday."

"He believed you?"

"Sure." Sally tried to charm the Trailsman with a quivering smile, but it dissolved under his glare.

She was doubtlessly telling the truth. Amos Win-

14

field wasn't given to questions. Over the years, Fargo had worked with Amos, for Amos, and over Amos countless times. He knew full well that Amos Winfield was never contrary. When the men under Amos got contentious or lazy, Amos just ambled along and did half their work himself. When things got real bad, Amos just handed over whatever pay he felt the miscreant deserved, and pointed back East.

For the first time, Fargo understood why Amos had turned down the five-thousand-dollar bonus being offered for safe delivery of a wagon train from here to Denver. In a normal summer, Winfield made the trip three or four times, but Winfield didn't have any talent for leading men. Experienced men followed Winfield because he knew his business, and greenhorns did as they were told because Amos was as large as an ox. They obviously believed that if Amos ever got riled, he would tear them all to pieces and stack them up for kindling.

Yet, in all the years the Trailsman had known Amos, he had never seen the wagon master get riled; he had never even heard of Amos raising his voice. Fargo had never heard Amos curse, a real phenomenon in a man who had started out as a bullwhacker, since oxen didn't understand any other language.

Although Winfield did have a frightening way of shoving an ox aside as if it were a yearling lamb, Fargo always suspected that Amos apologized to the oxen afterward. God knew, Amos hardly ever talked to men. Amos ruled with size and silence, but the men on this trip would need special instructions.

The army was giving escort to all westbound trains, but that had merely created a logjam of freighters waiting their turn. In the past couple of weeks, with the troopers riding out to check on one reported attack after another, there just hadn't been any escorts available. So if Fargo was going to get his consignment of mining equipment and assorted perishables through before the end of September, he was going to have to bypass the army.

The Trailsman believed that Amos could have got the train through on his own. But getting this train through was going to take bluster and persuasion and bullying—commands, demands, and perseverance. It was going to take more words than Amos had uttered in the last decade.

The crew would have to be as disciplined as an army; they would have to stand extra watches, miss sleep, miss meals, and be wary every minute. They would need a leader with a special kind of will, a man who could demand that the men watch their step every inch of the way. Skye Fargo had that sort of iron will—except when it came to women, he thought self-deprecatingly.

"Goddammit, why did Amos have to listen to you?" Fargo complained.

"Maybe because he likes me," Sally suggested.

"Are you claiming that you and Amos . . . ?" Fargo demanded, skewering her with his lake-blue glare.

"No, of course not," Sally whimpered, hugging herself with trembling arms while she scooted backward as if she could escape Fargo's penetrating scowl. "Amos isn't that kind of man."

But the Trailsman couldn't help but wonder whether Sally's strange pride-filled boast was a slip on her part. Surely she wasn't that stupid. No, who was he kidding? Sally had been stupid enough to start this confession.

She could have told Fargo that he'd been ill during those missing days. Or she could have kept her mouth shut. Well, maybe not, Fargo admitted. He hoped that he knew at least that much about her. But what did he really know?

Maybe she had merely contrived to cast the blame on Webster and McCormick. Maybe it wasn't them at all. Maybe she was protecting someone else. For the life of him, Fargo could think of no good reason for Webster and McCormick to want him delayed.

But Amos? What could a man really know about Amos? He was so damned quiet. No, Fargo tried to convince himself, Amos couldn't have anything to do with this predicament. But what if the freight company hadn't offered Amos the bonus? Suddenly Fargo was thinking all too clearly, and it was more unpleasant than his headache.

"Goddammit, answer me, woman. What's between you and Amos Winfield?"

"Nothing," Sally choked, gawking up at Fargo. "Nothing at all. I swear it. Besides, you know Amos."

"I thought I knew Amos."

"You know he's not like that with women."

"Like what?"

"I don't know," she snuffled miserably. "But you know. You know him. You know Amos."

"All I know is that for someone who chatters like a magpie, you sure do have trouble getting anything out."

"But you know," Sally asserted desperately. "Amos is . . . He's . . ."

"Dammit, quit your sniveling and say what you've got to say."

"Amos goes to Lilabeth's sometimes, like a lot of men. But he doesn't fall in love or anything. He just . . . He just . . ." Sally repeated, glancing up to meet Fargo's glowering gaze. "He just fucks," she blurted. "That's all. Him and me . . . we've . . . well, I've . . . Dammit, Skye, that's what I get paid for."

"So you're more than friends," Fargo accused.

"More than friends?" Sally repeated. "Amos is nice and all. I like him. He's always . . . I don't know. But how could we be more than friends? I don't think Amos Winfield has ever said three words to me at the same time. I guess we're not really friends at all. We're just . . ."

"Lovers," Fargo supplied.

"Oh, God," Sally burst out, winding up for another screeching session. "I knew I shouldn't have done it. Of all the people in the world to cross—the Trails-man." Sally laughed hysterically. Her nervous laughter screeched worse than the yowling of cats. "But it

17

was so much money," she whined. "And I had to get out. Can't you understand that?"

"Had to get out of what?"

"Lilabeth's," she shrieked. "I hate Lilabeth's."

It was bad enough that Fargo felt sorry for Sally, but even worse, he believed her. After what she had done, he had no reason to believe her, but he did.

"Damn you," Fargo swore, eyeing her angrily.

In actuality, she had caused very little damage. He was feeling better. The delay didn't really matter and the throbbing was settling to a dull headache. But here he was doubting Amos Winfield, who had never once done him a bad turn, because of this weepy jezebel. Besides, there was the principle of the matter. He couldn't let the woman think she could get away with putting Skye Fargo under just because it suited her.

"Please, Skye, I didn't mean to," Sally pleaded, ready to start a second screeching lament until the Trailsman fixed her with another ferocious scowl.

She deserved at least that much grief after what she had done. She deserved worse, but Fargo couldn't bring himself to dish it out. He couldn't remember the last three nights at all, but he remembered the first four.

There had never been a woman born who was as innocent as Sally looked. Fargo wanted to kick himself. He knew she whored at Lilabeth's place; that alone should have shown him that her innocent facade was all sham. But a week ago, when he'd ridden into town, hot and tired from the trail, he had made his first stop a saloon, and there she had been, not at all the sort of woman a man usually encountered in a saloon—no paint, no red satin, no black lace. A sweet face, nice breasts, and boundless enthusiasm.

She had acted as if she adored him, an important man, a famous tracker, a man with a reputation. And he had trusted her. He had been a damned fool.

Fargo gazed down coldly at Sally, pleased at her quivering, misty-eyed uncertainty. But Sally's expression changed. Her eyes got round as silver dollars as the corners of her mouth turned up in a little smile.

Fargo let go of the bedpost. "What in hell?" he mumbled. "Aw, shit," he cursed, realizing he was absolutely naked and had been dwelling on her female attributes in too much detail.

"No way, Sally. No way. It's not you. It's the herbs. It's the fresh air. It's because I've got to take a leak." Feeling more clearheaded, he stalked past Sally to grab his trousers off the dresser top. "Hey, did you say something about a thousand dollars?" he asked abruptly upon seeing his saddlebags in the corner.

Forgetting his nudity, Fargo changed course to grab the bulging saddlebags. He had his back to Sally, but out of the corner of his eye he caught the movement he'd been expecting. He wasn't near the fool she thought him.

He brought his Colt around. "Stop right there, honey."

With her robe bunched in one hand and her other hand on the floor, she was taking off in a half-crouch like the men from the fire companies did in their contests. "Oh," she puffed, still gazing longingly at the door as she dropped back on her ass.

"Going somewhere?" Fargo asked.

"No," she whispered.

"I thought not." He tossed his saddlebags on the bed and set the Colt next to the bags, where he could reach it in an instant. "You sit tight, sweetheart, and maybe I won't kill you. Then again, maybe I will. My headache is clearing, so I should be able to decide real soon."

2

The bank notes were more than enough money to pay any extra expense entailed by his delay—extra pay for the men, extra feed for the oxen. That was something that Fargo hadn't really believed, but Sally had indeed stuffed a thousand dollars in his saddlebags, although she obviously hadn't meant to stick around and explain why.

Frowning down at the bills in his hand, Fargo realized that if Sally's share was the same, Webster and McCormick were out two thousand dollars for a three-day lead that gained them nothing, since the problem this summer wasn't when you could get to Denver, it was whether you could get to Denver at all.

It didn't make sense. Although the Trailsman didn't ordinarily like to deal with big trains, he had even offered to combine trains with Webster and McCormick. More than three dozen wagons and a caravan got unwieldy, but under these circumstances, extra guns had seemed prudent.

Besides, Webster had hired some of the hardest-looking teamsters Fargo had ever seen. It stood to reason that the better freighters weren't making the trip this summer—not with the Sioux, Arapaho, and Cheyenne all on the warpath.

But a shortage of good men didn't make it advisable to hire misfits. And since Webster and McCormick hadn't seemed any more inclined than the Trailsman to wait for an army escort, Fargo had actually been worried about them, especially after seeing that crew. He had offered to combine trains because he'd thought that without someone like himself in charge, Webster and McCormick's crew was bound to rob them blind.

Fargo rubbed his sore shoulder. That's what came of trying to do someone a favor. He glanced out the window to see a clear, dry day in Leavenworth City, Kansas. Somewhere out there Fargo had thirty-six men, thirty wagons, and 350 oxen waiting for him.

He jammed the bank notes back into his saddlebag. He wasn't sure it was strictly ethical to keep them—money paid to sabotage an expedition he was in charge of—but keeping them made a hell of a lot more sense than giving them back to Sally.

"Don't you even think it," Fargo warned, noting that Sally's wistful regard was resting on the door once again. "I'm not through with you yet."

She turned her woeful, red-rimmed eyes on him. Just when Fargo had come to depend on her whining to keep him properly irritated, she didn't say a word.

What in hell had she expected to gain from giving him a thousand dollars, anyway? Fargo wondered. Thinking on it just plagued him with new suspicions, since Sally did know Amos, likely better than she claimed.

A top wagon master made about two hundred dollars a month. Fargo wasn't at all sure that Amos had been offered the big bonus, since Amos wasn't too voluble on the subject, or on any other subject, for that matter.

Maybe Amos had hoped that by leaving without Fargo, he could collect the bonus himself. Maybe Amos and the train were already gone. Fargo didn't like to believe his friend would do that to him, but maybe it was even fair. Amos had devoted years of his life to the freighting business.

Fargo had merely assumed Amos had been offered first crack at this job. But if Amos hadn't been offered the opportunity to earn the five-thousand-dollar bonus that went with this expedition, he might have been a little irked—and rightfully so, since he had always been good and true to Sampson and Sons, Traders, the outfit financing the journey.

On the other hand, Fargo seldom worked the big commercial trains, since the money men were always coming up with new ways to plague the honest workingman. Alexander Majors, one of the biggest commercial freighters, actually made his employees stand and take an oath that they wouldn't drink, curse, gamble, or mistreat animals while in his employ. To top it off, they had to swear that they would at all times comport themselves like gentlemen or else willingly forfeit their pay.

Although Fargo agreed that resting a day every week made sense, Majors' notion that it had to come on the Sabbath was wholly idiotic. It couldn't do a man's soul any good to have to bend the commandments and take to murdering Indians because he had been forced to lay over right where they had a perfect ambush plotted.

As far as Fargo was concerned, Majors' lamentable notions ruined the business of freighting. As was the way with idiotic notions everywhere, Majors' peculiar ideas were spreading to companies that had been sensible.

Then there was Amos. He didn't curse, he didn't gamble, and he didn't abuse men or animals. As far as Fargo knew, in his business dealings Amos Winfield had always lived up to any code that Majors or the Trailsman might want to impose. Although it was possible that Majors wouldn't agree, since even Amos bent the rules considerably. But all in all, just for remembering that there were rules that were supposed to apply after a man was out of the sight and hearing of company officials, Amos was worthier than most wagon masters. Fargo had always thought that Amos was as good a man as he'd ever come across.

Until now. A week ago, the Trailsman would have trusted Amos with his life, his money, his saddlebags, even his Ovaro. But now doubts nipped at him like red ants.

22

How was a man supposed to judge Amos? Amos wasn't like anybody else.

Sally did strike Fargo as sincere in her shrillness, if nothing else. He would almost swear she was telling the truth. But there was no figuring women. Women generally had more principles than men, but their principles were so adaptable. He supposed he would have gotten a lot colder on many a night if that wasn't the case, but it was still exasperating.

"I don't get it," Fargo grumbled.

"What?" Sally murmured.

He swung to face her. "You claim Webster and McCormick gave you this money. But why? Why did they go to all this trouble?"

"Webster said they wanted to get there first."

"But the point isn't to get there first," Fargo complained. "The point is to get there at all—without losing any men or wagons, and as few oxen as possible."

"Then why did they do this?"

"Good God, woman, that's what I'm asking you."

"How would I know?"

"You're the one who works for them."

"Oh, no, Skye, I wouldn't have done it if I hadn't known you could catch up. You're the best. You're famous."

"Jesus Christ, can't you understand? I don't give a damn if I catch up. What difference does it make? As long as I get to Denver by the end of September, I get paid the same, and the freighting company gets paid the same."

"But, Skye, they paid me two thousand dollars to keep you here. There must be some reason."

"I know that," he objected, his patience worn to a frazzle. He seized the walnut ball on the bedpost as if he meant to crush it while fixing Sally with a look he normally saved to make gunmen tremble. "But this is Winfield's money, isn't it?" he snapped, hoping to trap her.

"I don't know," she sputtered. "Is that what you

23

think? You think Amos is working for Webster and McCormick? That thought never crossed my mind."

"No, I don't think that," Fargo objected. "I think Amos is working with you."

"Me?" she squealed. "But I was working for Webster and McCormick. Although not really, Skye. Like I said, I knew you'd win. Honest, I knew. I'd never, I wouldn't, I couldn't, I really never, ever . . ." She sailed off on a high note the way most people did when they tried to sing "Dixie."

Fargo winced. "Would you quit that? Keep it up, honey, and you'll need to change your name to Jenny, because you sure bray like one."

He stepped to the window, but stayed beside the frame to remain concealed from view as he studied the street below. It teemed with men, wagons, oxen, mules, and horses, but nothing seemed unusual.

"I can't figure it," he said. "It's not like a normal year when the wagons are needed back here to get in another trip. As far as most everybody's concerned, the Great Platte River Road is closed for the summer. The Indians are playing for high stakes out there. It's too damn easy to lose your cargo, your wagons, your oxen, and your teamsters.

"What do you think I'm doing here?" Fargo scanned the crowd below. "I don't usually do this sort of thing. Freighting's not bad work, but it's pretty routine and it can get downright tedious. But they wanted somebody who knows Indians. I know Indians."

When Fargo turned back around, Sally was gazing at him with an expression so forlorn that he almost felt sorry for her again. He told himself he was crazy. After what she had done, he should have tossed her out the window.

But it was hard to ignore a woman so forthright. Her eyes focused right on what interested her most, which fortunately was no longer standing at attention as if it was a common foot soldier and she was commander-in-chief.

"Dammit, do you know what you did to me?" Fargo

demanded. "Laudanum. Whiskey. Belladonna. Herbs. You could have killed me."

Sally tilted her head back. Her chin shook as she nodded gravely. "I'm sorry," she mumbled.

"And then there's Amos," he complained. "Amos is one of my best friends, and you've made me think some of the worst things about him."

"I didn't mean to," she whimpered.

"Oh, hell," Fargo muttered. "You know something? You really are a bitch."

Sally took in a long sniffling breath that made her chest heave in a way that couldn't be resisted.

"But since you are in heat . . ."

Sally's questioning look evolved into a full-fledged smile accompanied by giggles. She stood and took a step toward him. "Oh, Skye, I'm so glad you don't hate me. I was so scared you would." Her smile faded as her gaze grew ardent. "You won't be sorry," she assured him.

"I'm already three days late," he mused. "What's another hour?"

"I want to make things up to you," she whispered. Sidling up against him, Sally slid her hand between them, and her fingers locked possessively around his organ.

Her other hand rose to untie the blue ribbon that held her curls in place, but Fargo reached back and helped her with that. So she started undoing the bone buttons of her flowered housecoat, revealing a magnificent pair of breasts that rose firmly, growing nipples high and pointing up, as if they were imploring the Trailsman to pay attention to them. He eased back a bit, to give himself room, and bent his neck to savor the buds, one at a time.

The short woman's arms were stretched, but she kept her stroking hold of Fargo's shaft. "Mmmm," she purred. "I want that."

Fargo wasn't of a mind to argue, so he edged forward, easing her back toward the bed. It caught her behind her knees. She toppled back, her robe aflutter because it still draped her shoulders and arms.

He had only a moment of indecision. Should they pause and finish removing the robe? Hell, no. As Sally fell on the bed, her silken cleavage soothed along his pulsing desire. Then her lips brushed before gravity took over, and her brown curls led the way to the coverlet.

Almost as if his shaft was leading the way, Fargo plunged atop her. She had arched her hips and was ready with a target he couldn't miss. With one deep thrust, Fargo was home.

"My God," Sally gasped. Her eager flush obscured those freckles, and those innocent brown eyes now displayed a wanton desire that started there and trembled down through her body. When it reached her center, all sorts of pleasant pulsations began to caress Fargo's shaft. And when it spread some more, her thighs rose and clamped tight around Fargo's torso.

She had surprising force in those short legs. For a moment, he couldn't even thrust. He had to wiggle a bit to give her the idea that a man needed some room to act.

Sally caught on and Fargo began stroking in and out, almost tentatively, because it felt so good inside that hot moist cavern that he didn't want to back out, even a little. But if a man didn't back out, he couldn't get the pleasure of returning, could he?

Then Fargo forgot all about thinking as their unspoken rhythm took over. Sally started to sound pretty religious, with a lot of loud gasping talk about God and heaven. Fargo paid it no mind. He felt free, free of the concerns about caravans and Indian uprisings, free of the worries about who might be trying to delay him and why, free of the muddled thinking this woman had inflicted on him. All that was important was getting as much of himself as he could inside warm, willing Sally.

He exploded. About ten seconds later, when he was

still pumping ecstasy, she did, too, in a wild screaming frenzy that should have broken the bed. After that, things got really wild. It was a good three hours before Fargo could summon the will and the energy to do what had to be done.

As Sally began a nap of contentment, Fargo made his way out. He stood on the stoop of a small white-washed frame house, with his fist raised to pound a second time when the door swung open.

"Skye," a hoarse voice rasped.

Before the Trailsman knew what was happening, two huge arms encircled him, mashing his face against a giant armpit. A massive hand slammed against his shoulder. Instinctively, Fargo went for his Colt, but the squeeze was too tight, his arm was trapped. For a moment, Fargo relaxed inside the bruising bear hug. Then he tensed his shoulders and twisted.

He was released so quickly he staggered, but his Colt was out. "What in hell?" Fargo spat, eyeing Amos Winfield warily.

Although Fargo had been almost positive his assailant was Amos, since the only other creature he knew of with a grip quite like Winfield's was a killer grizzly that rampaged up near the Canadian border, he hadn't wanted to believe it. The Trailsman surreptitiously stretched his lean torso and shrugged his crushed shoulders without letting the Colt stray from its mark.

Outside, Winfield's frame house had looked like a cottage. Inside, it was a trapper's cabin, one moderate-size room with a rough-hewn table and makeshift chairs. The bed was supported by a frame of unpeeled logs and covered with a buffalo robe. Several rifles were racked above it, but Amos didn't go for one.

Fargo relaxed as his lake-blue eyes settled on Winfield once again. "I think you've got some explaining to do."

But Amos merely gaped at the Colt, his pale-blue eyes wide with surprise. Color surged into the ruddy cheeks above his wild red beard. He stepped back a pace and his shoulders slumped. His gaze shifted nervously as if he wasn't able to look Fargo in the eye.

Everything about Winfield's posture was hangdog. He would have looked like a whipped mongrel, except he probably weighed more than a Mexican burro. Although Fargo had often suspected that Amos was softer than he looked, cringing wasn't like him.

Instantly, the Trailsman recognized that Amos was embarrassed. "You were worried about me," he said, realizing that Winfield's bear hug hadn't been a vicious assault; it had been a crazed greeting.

"Goddammit, Amos. Were you trying to get yourself killed?" Fargo pontificated, feeling more chagrined himself as he reholstered his Colt. Kicking aside a chair, he sat down and uncoiled his more-than-six-foot length.

Amos was the only man in the world who made Skye Fargo feel small. Even with his head hanging low, Amos was as massive as Scott's Bluff, and he had a way of filling a room, not only with his bulk but also with his presence. Even when you weren't looking, you knew Amos was there, too damn big to be ignored, too damn quiet to be comfortable with. Winfield's mortification only made the feeling worse.

Dark curtains fluttered at the windows, blocking out the sight and sound of Leavenworth while an overhead lantern shed reasonable light on the rustic room. Amos turned to the bubbling kettle on the stove. "Coffee?" he asked.

"Sure," Fargo agreed. "So, what have you been doing?" he asked, peering up at what could be seen of Winfield's generously bearded face.

Winfield's shoulder-length yellow hair contrasted bizarrely with his wild red beard. Since Amos was so big and quiet, some men concluded that he was as stupid as a draft animal, but Fargo knew better. There was intelligence in those pale-blue eyes. Winfield didn't comment readily, but he watched everything going on around him.

Winfield sat down across from Fargo. He dwarfed his chair. He dwarfed the table as he propped his elbows on it. The enormous hands circling his over-sized coffee mug made the cup look like a toy out of a little girl's tea set.

"Told the men you was delayed checking out an inventory problem," Amos announced gruffly. "Been making 'em drill on those Henry sixteen-shooters Sampson supplied."

"You didn't tell them I'd disappeared?"

"Nope," Amos denied.

"Just kept them too busy to question my absence," Fargo observed.

"Yep."

"Why?"

"Huh?"

"Why didn't you want them to know I was missing?" Fargo challenged.

"Thought you'd tell 'em what you wanted 'em to know."

Silence settled in. With the stove going the room was too warm. While Amos stared down at the cup in his hands, Fargo perspired. Winfield was impossible to read. His beard almost covered his face.

The most surprising thing about Winfield was his age. He couldn't be more than thirty, but he seemed as much a fixture of the West as the Rockies. That's where Amos came from.

At least, old-timers claimed that a reclusive mountain man, even less given to talk than Amos, had shown up south of the Bayou Salade, toting a blond woman along with him in about 1825 or '26, back when that part of the Rockies had been part of Mexico, and the laws had been such that trappers who wandered in didn't brag on it. Then there had been a lot of Utes, some Jicarilla Apache, a few squawmen, and a couple of Spanish families in that four thousand or so square miles of what was now Colorado Territory. As the story went, the couple roamed that area

29

for fifteen years, carrying with them an ever-increasing passel of yellow-haired children, until they just disappeared.

Whether the tale was true or not, in 1849 a couple of Utes arrived in Santa Fe, offering to trade a big yellow-haired boy for something more useful. The boy went to a group of high-minded citizens in exchange for two blankets and a mule.

The citizens had no idea what to do with the boy, who seemed to understand English well enough, even though he never did utter a word of it. Finally a wagon master named Winfield came along and decided the boy might make a great bullwhacker, for the kid was as big as an ox. Once the senior Winfield found out that the boy's incomprehensible Ute served as well as the more conventional swear words to prod the animals down the trail, Amos was more or less adopted and named.

With such a background, Amos Winfield might have become a living legend, but fame required some self-promotion. At least that's why Fargo figured Winfield's wasn't well-known. After all, Kit Carson was forever telling stories, Joe Meek was collecting his memoirs, Jim Beckwourth was a consummate liar, and even the Trailsman wasn't above spinning a tale or two if someone else furnished whiskey.

Although Amos had eventually started speaking English on occasion, he certainly hadn't taken to boasting. Winfield's silence was burdensome. Fargo wanted to sit it out, figuring that when the quiet got to be too much for Amos, the man would start gibbering like most men would. But Amos seemed to be relaxing. Quiet didn't get to him; talking did.

"Goddammit! Aren't you even going to ask where I've been?" Fargo demanded.

"Is it my business?"

"Hell, yes, it's your business," Fargo retorted. "I'm the trail boss and I've been missing for three whole days. Don't you find that in the least bit curious?"

"Well, uh, sure, but . . ." Amos shifted uncomfortably and his weight came down on one elbow and tilted the whole table. "I'm sorry," he said, jumping up to grab a towel.

Fargo could feel the floorboards bounce in protest at Winfield's bounding steps. As Amos whirled to mop up spilled coffee, Fargo scooped his cup out of the way. Amos was obviously still embarrassed, and he was clumsy in his humiliation. The man was too big to be kept inside, Fargo thought. Sitting at a table with his Ovaro would make as much sense.

"Goddammit, Amos. Sit back down," Fargo commanded irritably. "A little spilt coffee isn't worth stomping this place apart over. What's gotten into you, anyway?" he asked suspiciously. "You generally don't move any faster than those lumbering beasts of yours."

"Nothing," Amos answered sullenly.

Nobody with any sense would continue to rail at Amos the way Fargo was. But Fargo wasn't feeling sensible as he seethed with suspicion. "Maybe, you're not curious about where I've been," the Trailsman went on. "But I'm going to tell you anyway. I've been with your girlfriend, Sally Mason. She drugged me and kept me in bed for three whole days."

Winfield's mouth dropped open and he gawked at Fargo. "You're that good?" he blurted.

"What?" Fargo snapped. "Oh, for God's sake, Amos. She didn't keep me for that. She claims she kept me in bed because Webster and McCormick paid her to. What I want to know is—if that's the truth."

Amos nodded thoughtfully. "All right," he assented. "How do you want me to find out?"

"Oh, to hell with it," Fargo muttered. "When do you think we can leave?"

"Dawn."

"Dawn? You mean the wagons are all packed? The men are all outfitted? The livestock assembled? The teams chosen? Everything?"

"Sure."

Sure, Amos told him, as if that were ordinary. While the Trailsman had been abed, Amos had been doing all the work. If anybody but Amos had been second in command, Fargo's absence would have meant a week of reorganizing before they could leave. It was time he turned his mistrust to someone else, Fargo decided.

But when he tried to imagine just one middling reason for Webster and McCormick to spend two thousand dollars to delay him, he couldn't.

3

Stomping hooves, lowing oxen, nickering horses, the low voices of two men exchanging places for the night watch, the smells of livestock, manure, and big bluestem. Something was wrong. Listening intently, Fargo rolled over in his bedroll.

He hadn't slept well. This was their second week out, but he had been plagued by bad feelings since leaving Leavenworth. This wasn't the first time he'd been awakened by noises that didn't seem quite right.

There it was again, an ordinary low whinny, not so different from the rest, except the direction. The Trailsman scrambled into his pants and boots.

"How's it going?" he asked a guard.

"Fine, sir."

Still pulling on his shirt, Fargo stood outside the wagon enclosure, scanning the trail and the wall of grass far beyond it. Barely visible by the light of the quarter moon, a silhouette hulked across the mile-wide swath of the trail.

"Where's he going?" Fargo asked the guard, just as the distant figure disappeared into the seven-foot grass.

"To relieve himself, I suspect, sir."

Fargo was already several yards away. "Next time, don't suspect, ask," he flung back without taking his eyes off the spot where Amos Winfield had disappeared. The Trailsman followed.

Fargo had to move slowly in the tallgrass since there was no way to mute his noise as he inched blindly through the tangling stems. His task seemed akin to looking for a needle in a haystack. Or perhaps it was

33

more like searching for Indians in a wheatfield at midnight, in that it was not merely foolish, it was downright hazardous.

If Amos heard Fargo, he would likely shoot, which was only reasonable: that was what the Trailsman would do in his place. But Fargo wasn't about to shout a greeting. He wanted to know what Amos was up to, because he didn't for a minute believe that Amos was wandering so far just to relieve himself, not when 350 oxen were already stinking up camp.

Fargo paused to listen. Far behind, the oxen stomped, snorted, and generally complained; they always seemed so placid by day, so restless by night. A few men's voices wafted over. The horses weren't quite as noisy, but they made their presence known.

Close by, the grasses whispered as they rustled, but otherwise silence reigned. Greenhorns always griped about that unnerving silence. A testimony to the vastness of the grasslands, the quiet inspired loneliness and desolation more readily than the most maudlin of ballads.

The prairies stretched from east to west for more than five hundred miles and ran pretty much unbroken from the Dakota Territory to Texas, a great grassland sheltering Pawnee, Cheyenne, Arapaho, Sioux, wolves, snakes, skunks, and various vermin. Yet none seemed as threatening as the sheer enormity of it all.

Silence and space, they were what made men feel lost, Fargo reflected. He had no idea where he was going, but he was fairly sure he was the noisiest creature going there. July had been hot. The sun-dried grass swished around him and crackled under his feet.

He couldn't see his hand in front of his face. He doubted he could find anything that didn't reach out and nab him first. Yet every time the grass waved around him, he knew he was making enough commotion to alert anyone looking for him.

Fargo paused again to listen. If he was creating such a ruckus, then surely, considering the size of the man, Amos should have been thundering. But Fargo couldn't hear anything besides the distant sounds of camp and the whisper of the grass.

In the vast darkness a mile from his horse, the Trailsman understood why greenhorns feared the prairies, but he didn't share their fear. The tallgrass prairie didn't scare him, it annoyed him. It removed the advantage of being an expert tracker. He couldn't see a blessed thing, and one match could turn the grass into his funeral pyre. A few trees lurked in the grass, but for the most part, grass didn't snag pieces of hair and fiber. Unlike soil or mud, grass didn't hold a footprint. Tallgrass blocked the light so you couldn't see the earth. Grasslands, especially at night, made an expert tracker feel like a greenhorn.

Abruptly, a thrashing resounded through the grass. By its speed as it thrashed by Fargo, it had to be a startled rabbit. The Trailsman took a step forward. A flower pod slapped his face. He jerked back. A bur oak stabbed his side. Even though the grass all looked pretty much the same from the road, it wasn't.

With enormous effort, Fargo suppressed his irritation and crept forward again, angling toward the area the rabbit had fled. The going was slow. The grass wisped across his face like cobwebs. The leafy bases of the big bluestem grabbed at his boots.

But Winfield would recognize the sound of a man walking through the grass, so Fargo resisted the urge to hurry. Separating the stems with his arms, he planted his footsteps carefully. Still he seemed to make a powerful amount of racket.

Finally, he heard low, sonorous, barely audible voices. Fargo edged forward until he was merely a city block away. The voices were louder, but he couldn't make out the words. He inched closer, settling each step as if he were walking on quicksand.

Fargo didn't want to fire on Winfield, not until he knew more, and he sure as hell didn't want Winfield shooting at him, but even as he drew too close for comfort, he couldn't make out the words of Winfield's conversation. Then, it came to him: the words were in

Cheyenne. The Trailsman knew a bit of Cheyenne, but Winfield and his companion were yammering too fast for him.

Slowly, Fargo turned and eased back toward camp. Every yard gained took an eternity. It was so dark that he might as well have been blindfolded. A root grabbed him, then a gopher hole, then another root. Each time he lurched blindly and clutched at the grass on either side, which served no purpose whatsoever except to annoy him more. After about a mile, his patience snapped.

Fargo bounded forward and sprinted. Most men walked; the Trailsman bolted. Any man disturbed by his tumult would take him for a jackrabbit, a white-tailed deer, or a coyote, he decided. Instead of slowing for the trail, he streaked across it.

"Davis," he shouted as he neared the wagons. "Call out the extra watch."

The men assumed their stations smartly. Within minutes their loaded Henrys covered the range outside the train's enclosure. The irony of it all was that Amos had trained them. He'd drilled them all on the new Henrys. He'd warned them that the repeating rifles were susceptible to dust and muck. He'd run spot checks to make sure the weapons were clean. And Fargo knew it had all been done right, because he had checked it himself.

"Don't fire unless I say so," Fargo ordered.

The wait seemed interminable as dawn lightened the sky from black to darkest blue. Indians generally attacked by day, but they stole by night. The Trailsman had no intention of being ambushed or robbed. Across the trail the grasses shuttered.

"Hold your fire," Fargo shouted as Amos emerged alone. "Hold your fire, but keep your places."

Abandoning the refuge of the wagons, the Trailsman walked toward Winfield. His eyes scanned the blue-stem, his vision pierced the gloom of the trail to the east and to the west. He didn't see anything unusual in any direction.

"Where've you been?" Fargo asked, halting several yards away.

"Out there," Winfield answered, waving his arm toward the seven-foot wall of grass.

"Why?"

"I heard something."

"And?" Fargo urged.

Winfield gazed beyond the Trailsman's shoulder, but he didn't so much as flinch at the sight of the Henrys aimed his way. "So that was you rampaging out there," he commented. "Thought it was a white-tail."

"I think you have some explaining to do."

"Looks like it," Amos agreed.

"Well, goddammit, start explaining."

"They're not coming. Leastways not yet. You can call off the guard."

"I'm supposed to take your word for that?" Fargo demanded.

Surprise stiffened Winfield's massive torso as his gaze shifted from the rifles to Fargo. "Yes."

Fargo grunted as he turned back toward the wagons. He didn't like it one damned bit, but he trusted Winfield's word. "Fool," he muttered to himself as he stalked back to the train.

"You can cancel the double watch," he told Davis. "But those who stay on better keep alert."

The Trailsman strode toward the fire. He wanted to see Winfield's face when he talked to him. But when Winfield stepped forward, his flamboyant beard shielded his features. His shoulder-length blond hair glowed an eerie orange in the firelight.

"What in hell's going on, Amos?"

"Nothing," the huge man answered as he squatted before the fire. He grabbed a tin cup from the tarp that spread in reach of the fire, then took up the huge kettle of coffee resting in the coals. "Want some?" he asked.

"No. Yes. I don't know. Dammit, Amos. What were you doing out there?"

"Talking."

"To who? Why? Damn you, I need answers."

"Skye, I'm trying," Amos protested. He settled back on his ass with his elbows propped on his knees and his cup clutched in his hands. In no hurry to satisfy Fargo's curiosity, he gazed into the fire.

"Damn," Fargo muttered. Then, recalling that prodding Amos when he got in one of his moods was about as useful as prodding an oak, he poured himself a cup of coffee and settled down to wait.

"Lone Wolf," Amos finally answered. "I was talking to Lone Wolf. He's pretty well connected. Thought I could talk him into giving us safe passage. I couldn't. He couldn't."

"Then they're going to attack?"

"Don't know. I guess they will if they do. Won't if they don't." Amos leaned toward the fire. His head was down, his back was bent, he looked as though he carried the weight of the world on his wide shoulders.

What did Fargo really know about him? He knew that Winfield hauled freight in the summer; he had no idea what he did in the winter. The fluency of his talk with Lone Wolf had been a shock to the Trailsman.

"Amos, you've got to help me. I'm trying to trust you, but I can't believe you just ran into that Indian out there. When did you set that meeting up? Why did you set it up?"

"I didn't. Lone Wolf's always out there. He finds me."

"Damn you, Amos, why? What am I supposed to believe after I get drugged by your whore, waylaid for three days, then find you conspiring with an Indian? Why didn't you take the five-thousand-dollar bonus for this trip? I thought maybe you didn't feel up to dealing with the Indians, as troublesome as they've been lately, but—"

"But you was right," Amos objected. "I can't fight Cheyenne. You order it, I'll do it. But I can't choose to do it." Amos sighed before quaffing the rest of his coffee. "Guess it'll come to that, too," he ruminated, more to the fire than to Fargo. "Lone Wolf says the warriors are so riled, there's no talking to 'em. Don't matter who I am."

"And just who in hell are you?" Fargo chafed. "Who's Lone Wolf? What do the Cheyenne have to do with you?"

"They're kin."

"Kin?" Fargo exploded. "You're whiter than I am. I'm a quarter Cherokee. You've got hair the color of daisies. Your eyes show hardly any color at all. I know you were raised by Utes, but the Utes are enemy to the Cheyenne. So how can you be kin to the Cheyenne?"

"Married one."

"A wife? Dammit, I've known you for nigh on ten years, Amos. Since when did you have a wife?"

"Always. Married her first trip up from Santa Fe. But she died last year."

Betrayed, he felt betrayed. It was silly, Fargo suspected, but he had known Amos a long time. They had ridden together, eaten together, spent many a quiet evening by a campfire together. Maybe Amos didn't talk much, but Fargo had always felt he knew him.

But he didn't know Amos at all, he realized. The man was an enigma, a mystery, a stranger. So how could he trust him?

That was Fargo's other problem: he did trust Amos. Whether it was foolish or wise, considering Sally, Lone Wolf, and all of Winfield's other surprises, Fargo trusted him instinctively.

"Amos?" he asked tiredly. "Why didn't you ever mention you had a wife?"

"Didn't think folks would understand."

"Me too, huh?" Fargo asked resentfully. "You figured me for one of those folks who wouldn't understand? Why, Amos? Because she was Cheyenne? You know I wouldn't have judged on that. There's lots of folks who call me a breed." Fargo paused and then smiled, trying to take the edge off his anger. "Although not many call me that to my face."

"Don't it bother you some that you scare men?" Amos asked gruffly.

"No, not particularly."

"Bothers me," Amos said. "Grown men are afraid of me. And it's always been that way, 'cept for the Cheyenne. Ain't hard for a man my size to impress warriors, for Indians do love fierceness. Not sure I was born for it, but it's better than being . . ." Amos broke off and stared into the fire.

"What?" Fargo urged.

"Alone."

The wind picked up. It was warm, but its voice gave a chill as it moaned across the plains. A sudden gust caught at the fire and made the orange flames dance.

"I like being alone," Fargo commented.

"Sure you do," Amos bristled. "You ride into town and the ladies run up to kiss you and the gents all come out to kiss your ass. I ride in, they back off. Alone ain't so bad if you give it a break once in a while. But you just try it as a steady diet. It's worse than mule meat."

Fargo almost laughed. He had seldom heard Amos get even a trifle irritable, had never once heard him use sarcasm before. "Hell, maybe you should shave," Fargo suggested. "Maybe folks just aren't sure it's only a man under all that fur."

"Maybe I will."

"Amos, I was kidding. For God's sake, why do you take folks so seriously?"

"You don't understand," Amos insisted.

Fargo tried smiling. Usually his smile worked wonders. A woman had once told him he could use his smile to charm fishing worms out of the ground, and even men seemed a bit more at ease when he bothered to smile.

The Trailsman was tall, lean, rangy muscle. He wore a Colt at his side, carried a ready throwing knife, and never looked away from a fight when he felt one was due. He had seen more than most men ever would see or ever wanted to see, and it showed. If his smile could raise worms, his frown could send them burrowing again. Fargo frightened people, plenty of people.

But as many as Amos? No. Amos was a wonder of nature. He weighed at least three hundred pounds, and not a bit of it was fat. His biceps were bigger than many men's waists. His shoulders spread too wide to go straight through a door. He cast a shadow so big it seemed to squash the spirit of most men.

Fargo had never thought much about loneliness. Being alone was something he chose, but he realized now how different it would be to have it chosen for him. He wasn't really much more of a talker than Amos, but glancing at the big man, sitting there with his shoulders hunched and his gaze fixed on the fire, the Trailsman felt compelled to say something.

"Hell," he said. "I know some settlers don't take kindly to white men marrying squaws, but there's no reason to listen to their bitching, Amos. It's folks like us who've made it safe for them."

"You still don't understand," Amos reiterated.

"Hell if I don't. I know times are changing," Fargo objected. "But there's nothing wrong with an Indian wife. Carson had two. Meek's still got one, and Bridger's wife is Shoshone. Then there's Beckwourth. To hear him tell it, he's got a bride or more in every Indian camp from Texas to Dakota. Amos, nobody important would have thought less of you for marrying a squaw."

"You don't understand," Amos insisted harshly. "I wasn't a squawman, Skye. I was Cheyenne."

He stood. Behind him the sky had lightened to the lead gray of dawn. His bulk towered. Winfield was as big as a grizzly and damned near as wild-looking with his shaggy long hair and flowing beard.

Fargo stared up at him. "Dear God," he muttered. "Red Bear?"

"Red Bear," Amos agreed. "You still so understanding, Skye?" There was mockery in Winfield's gruff tone, and other things—despair, hopelessness, resignation.

Fargo turned and poured himself another cup of

coffee, since it didn't seem right to just sit there gawking at Amos. Red Bear, legend of the Pawnee, the Ute, and the Crow, an evil spirit who guided the Cheyenne. Fargo glanced back up at Amos. "I'm trying," he answered.

The sounds of rising men drifted Fargo's way, along with the smell of frying fatback from their fires. Already some of the bullwhackers and herders were trying to separate teams, and the oxen bellowed pitifully in anticipation of the new day. But for a long time after Amos walked away, Fargo just sipped at his coffee and mused.

Amos, stark naked, painted from head to toe with red ocher, with bear claws extending from his fingertips and a bear-claw necklace hanging across his furry chest. Amos leading the Cheyenne into battle. Amos carrying the ceremonial war lance decorated with beads and feathers and the scalps of Crow, Ute, Pawnee, and white men. Fargo couldn't imagine it. Yet Amos was Red Bear.

Red Bear was said to be half-grizzly, half-man. Red Bear tore his enemies apart with his claws and his teeth. It was said he boasted a shaft twice as large as mortal man's, a weapon he used to impale the women of his enemies. From his seed children sprang forth half-grown—fierce children, children with hair tipped by the sun, children who were cousins of the grizzly.

Fargo had seen one of those children once. The kid was practically worshiped by his band, but he had looked like an ordinary child to Fargo. The boy was a little big for his age and his hair was curiously streaky, but otherwise he was just a boy, although he definitely wasn't pure Indian. The boy was a half-breed, nothing more. Amos Winfield's half-breed.

Fargo tossed his cold coffee into the fire. It hissed and spit on the glowing coals. Never before had the differences between the culture of the white man and the culture of the red man seemed so huge to him.

Before, it had always seemed a given that Indians rode off to war mostly naked, but painted. It hadn't seemed remarkable that dog soldiers barked and snarled and bared their teeth. It hadn't seemed particularly relevant that in a lot of tribes the warriors imitated the mascot of their warrior societies. It hadn't seemed any more outlandish than a bugler and banners. Until Amos.

It was said Red Bear could tear the throat from a man with one savage bite while his claws tore into his victim's genitals and ripped them off. According to his adversaries, no enemy facing Red Bear ever departed for the happy hunting grounds a whole man; the enemies of Red Bear were doomed to wander eternity with ravaged souls.

It was making Fargo queasy to think so much about Red Bear on an empty stomach. He stood, stretched, and shook his head to clear it, then he walked out to the middle of the trail to loosen muscles tired from sitting.

The sky was full blue overhead without a cloud, but Fargo frowned as he scanned the trail ahead. He squinted. It didn't look like any more than the smoke of a cigar, but it was ahead.

The wagons were chained front to rear to make a protective enclosure for the livestock. The oxen hadn't yet settled into the routine; nor were the bullwhackers and herders any too efficient as yet. Inside the enclosure beasts milled and bawled. Fargo jumped over the chain and entered the melee.

Men were trying to wrestle their teams out of the fray. To little avail, they shouted, shoved, and swore. The first week on the trail, it took hours to get the teams sorted, hitched, and moving. This was the second week; they were getting better, but they were still a long ways from efficient.

Since Fargo had no patience with the absolute chaos the men and beasts managed to create, he had assigned the supervision of the task to Amos. He spotted the big man right away. Winfield stood in a snarl of oxen, pushing them apart, while a herder clung atop one of the beasts because it had been the only place to jump to avoid getting crushed.

The whole area was thick with dust. It smelled worse than an unlimed outhouse. And it was perilously overcrowded, worse than being in any city.

"Amos," Fargo bellowed, "I'm scouting ahead. Don't start the wagons till I get back."

The noises conflicting with Fargo's orders were overwhelming, but Amos heard him. "We'll wait," he roared back.

Fargo vaulted out of the arena and retrieved his pinto from where he'd picketed it near his bedroll. The haze on the horizon was still as wispy and pale as morning fog, but it was far more definite than it had been earlier. He rode west.

4

Gray gathered on the horizon like storm clouds. The fierce wind, straight out of the west, pushed directly into Fargo's face. The smell of smoke was unmistakable. "Shit." He spurred his Ovaro.

The Trailsman topped a low rise and saw the orange glow creep up behind waves of green-gold grass. The trail here was narrower than back at camp, but it was still far wider than any Main Street. He reined in and stared.

The days had been dry and the grass was high, but it was early for prairie fires. The ground was still damp compared to what it would be in another month or so. From the moment he had suspected fire, Fargo had hoped it wouldn't have had time to take hold, but he hadn't known then that the fire had been helped along.

The grass burned furiously on both sides of the trail; the fire had obviously been set. The arsonists had torched about fifty yards on the north and south sides of the road; it was burning too evenly to believe anything else. A warm wind blowing straight out of the west was no blessing, but at least it was keeping the blaze somewhat contained, although it spread a bit to the south.

Fargo headed back to camp. There wasn't time for a closer look. The fire was twenty to twenty-five miles from camp, more than a day's travel for the oxen, but not for flames. And the Trailsman had already been gone for an hour.

When Fargo arrived, men stood outside the enclosure, staring at the sky. It was grayer now, the heavy, ominous gray of thunderclouds.

"Jameson, you and Rogers unload one of the wagons. Davis, you and Scott find everything that can hold water. Maxwell and Sinclair, gather blankets. You, Thompson, fetch the shovels."

Fargo fired off more orders as he dismounted. He turned around. "Damn," he growled. In the west, the darkness had mounted as if the sun were in eclipse.

Amos stepped beside the Trailsman. "What should I do?"

"You know a way to turn the wind?"

"Why's it building so fast?" Amos asked. "Weren't there before daylight. Would have cast red glare. We'd have seen it."

If Fargo had nursed any suspicions about Winfield, they were quelled by the tone of perplexity in the huge man's speech as he stared at the gray cloud growing in the west.

"I know it's been dry," Amos pondered. "But my moccasins are still chilled from treading in grass last night. The prairie ain't dried out, Skye. Fire shouldn't be building like that."

"It had help. Probably a considerable amount of coal oil. And now it's got the wind."

"Help?" Amos spun and gaped at Fargo.

"Yes, help," Fargo roared. "Somebody set the blasted fire."

Winfield's huge body bristled. "You think me or Lone Wolf set it, don't you?"

"I didn't say that," Fargo protested.

"You didn't have to," Amos scoffed.

Winfield's yellow hair whipped across his face in the stiff breeze, and even his beard appeared to be heading east. Fargo stared beyond him at a blackening sky. He shouted more orders to the men. A wagon just loaded with barrels, canteens, and kettles headed for the river, half a mile away.

"You think I'm stupid, Skye?" Amos demanded. "Is that it? You think I ain't noticed you been accusing me of a lot of things I ain't done? And now you think I done this, don't you?"

"No, I don't," Fargo objected. "Jansen, get ten men ready to ride and fight it." Fargo strode through camp, stopping here and there to issue orders.

Amos followed at his heels.

"Make sure everybody's got food," Fargo told one of them. "And full canteens. And a knife."

"You're sure?" Amos asked.

"Yes, I'm sure," Fargo answered.

"I sure hope you're sure," Amos brooded. "Because, Skye, I swear I didn't have nothing to do with this. You got to believe me."

"Dammit, Amos. The truth is, maybe I should think you set it. Or I should at least think you encouraged Lone Wolf to set it. But I don't think that. There's just something about you. If I'd actually seen you out there with a torch and a bucket of coal oil, I probably still wouldn't think you set it. So there. Quit fretting about it and start worrying about this goddamned fire. All right?"

"Why? Worrying won't help."

"Damn you, Amos." Fargo led his Ovaro out to the road, searching anxiously for the sight of the wagon returning from the river. "In all the years I've known you, you've never been given to smart remarks. Why do you have to start with them now?"

"Don't know."

"If I leave you in charge of camp, you can handle it?"

"Sure."

"You said you couldn't fight Cheyenne. What happens if they come now?"

"I said I couldn't choose to fight Cheyenne. They come now, I got no choice. You go, Skye. Don't worry about the train."

"Okay," the Trailsman agreed as he swung aboard his Ovaro. He turned to face Amos; even from atop a horse Winfield didn't look small. "Amos, before I go, what's between us and that fire?"

"Lemuel Bittenhower's got a crude little stage stop. Lousy chow. Won't be helping you none, though. What with the stage not running, he's been in St. Joe tying one on. And there's some farms out there." Amos swept his arm wide, indicating all the grassland north of the trail. "They'll be watching to make sure it don't veer their way. Doubt they'll come help, though. Be too busy pulling water out of their wells and soaking their own roofs."

Fargo nodded. Asking Amos about the trail ahead had given him a peculiar feeling. Ordinarily, he knew more about the road he was on than anyone with him, but he hadn't swung up from Leavenworth to the Platte in several years. All the men on this trip had been across here more recently than Fargo. It was possible that some of them resented the Trailsman for that.

As he watched his men saddle their horses, Fargo wondered how many of them knew about the bonus. Then he wondered how those who did know felt about it—since there were obviously two ways of looking at it: either they felt more secure having the Trailsman along, or they felt Sampson had hired an outsider with a fancy reputation who didn't know half as much as they did about freighting.

Someone had set that fire. Eliminating Amos still left thirty-five men under Fargo's command who might have felt they had reason.

Fargo hated harboring suspicions about his own men, and yet suspicions nibbled at him. Last night hadn't been the first night he had come awake feeling that something was wrong in his camp. A feeling, whisperings, sounds in the night—those things didn't count for much in a camp housing several dozen men, hundreds of oxen, and twenty horses. But Fargo couldn't just ignore them, either.

"I suppose we could turn the train back," he commented, more to himself than to Amos. The Trailsman knew that it was the safest course, even as he admitted that he wasn't the one to take it. Someone had set a fire to stop him, and that kind of thing made him all the more determined to go on.

Amos turned and scowled at the road behind them. He folded his arms across his massive chest and looked as immovable as a butte.

"You're right," Fargo agreed to the unspoken message in Winfield's stance. "Turning the train would take every hand, assuming we wanted to get the wagons far enough away to matter. So if we turn back, we can't fight the fire at all. And then where would we be? Back at the start, with forty or fifty miles of burned forage ahead of us. We'd have hungry oxen dropping right and left. And I sure don't want to have to explain those kind of losses to Sampson."

"I don't know," Amos said with a worried look. "If it was me, I'd turn back. You, though? I really believe you'll put that fire out. But, Skye, the wind's up."

"Hell." Fargo laughed. "Better to go for broke and lose the whole damned train—if it comes to that—than to have to explain a few puny losses."

While the ten men chosen for fire detail checked their gear, the water wagon turned onto the main trail. Fargo quickly decided that the fire line couldn't be set more than five miles from camp. Any more than that, and the slow-moving water wagon wouldn't do them any good. But only five miles meant they'd have to make the line hold, which wouldn't be easy in this wind.

"Wait," Amos cried, ducking his head to remove a pouch that hung around his neck.

Meanwhile, Fargo raised his arm to signal to his men to move out. If he had been really observant in the past, Fargo decided, he would have noted just how much Indian paraphernalia Winfield sported: moccasins, a beaded knife case, quilled tobacco pouch, embroidered belt with buckskin fringe. But Indian doodads were sold at every trading post, and a lot of men wore them.

"Here," Amos said, holding out a small buckskin pouch. "No, don't open it."

"What is it?" Fargo asked, turning over the elaborately decorated bag, suddenly wondering if Winfield's wife had sewn all those beads in place.

"Luck. It's for luck." Amos looked solemn enough for a funeral. Crazy as it was, the beaded sack meant something to him.

Fargo slipped it around his own neck. "So you think I'll be needing this?"

"Can't hurt."

"Hell, no. And who knows? Maybe we'll get real lucky. Maybe the damned wind will blow the fire right out." Fargo dropped his arm, his men spurred their horses, and he followed, prompting the Ovaro to race ahead.

A scant fifteen minutes away from camp, Fargo signaled for the ten horsemen to dismount. The slow water wagon and its six men were still miles back, but there was no waiting for them.

"Grab your canteens and knives. Drink when you need to, but be thrifty. Now, spread out and start cutting."

The air was just fouled enough to make eyes water and noses itch when the Trailsman bent to his task along with his men, all in a line, each stationed several hundred feet from another so they didn't have to be too dainty with their knives.

"Damn," he muttered as he hacked at a woody mass growing in the grass. A backfire was the only solution, but with the wind raging against them, it didn't seem that they'd be able to establish a wide-enough safety corridor to risk lighting one.

As he ripped at the grass with his belt knife, the Trailsman thought of the stamps aboard wagons back at camp. They were huge, heavy hunks of metal used for crushing rocks. Practically indestructible, that's what they were, and it gave Fargo an idea. But it would take more than three hours to get those stamps to the fire line, and Fargo wasn't sure they had the time. He straightened.

Down in the grass, the wind didn't buffet the way it

had up on horseback, but the wind was notable, none-theless. The whole world was canting east. Fargo had managed to hack away maybe three square yards. Sweat poured off him and his eyes smarted. The first flecks of black ash drifted in front of Fargo. He knew from experience that ash would soon be coming like snow in a blizzard. The Trailsman went to inspect the others' progress.

As much as a barber needed a razor, the firefighters needed a plow. Hacking at the brush with knives made no more sense than tweezing a man's beard out hair by hair.

Rogers was surely the worst of the hackers. Fargo couldn't detect so much as a dimple in the area Rogers was supposed to be cutting. "Rogers," he bellowed. "Get over here." The grass shivered.

Satisfied that the teamster was answering his sum-mons, the Trailsman turned his attention to the horses. They were all there. The roan, the bay, the piebald mare, Fargo moved among them, crooning encourage-ment, patting one's head, scratching between anoth-er's ears. It wasn't too bad yet; the air was rank but not choking. Given how horses felt about fire, though, it was a miracle they all weren't halfway back to Leav-enworth by now.

With his bandanna clasped to his face, Rogers stag-gered from the brush, coughing and wheezing. The man's eyes were red and swollen, his skin was puffy, and the hand over the handkerchief was downright shaky.

The Trailsman glared at him. "You always that bad?" he asked coldly, because it was obvious the man wasn't just suffering from the smoke.

"Only when I'm down in it," Rogers gasped.

"And when I picked you for fire line you didn't think you'd be down in it?"

"I didn't think—"

"No, you didn't," Fargo interrupted.

Hay fever, it was a piddling affliction, hardly worth mentioning, until a man was forced to work in the midst of the tall grass. Because of their pride, herders and vaqueros often failed to mention that they had it. Suddenly, Fargo remembered all of the reasons that usually made him choose to work alone. A five-thousand-dollar bonus wasn't worth the aggravation of bossing a crew, especially a bonus that, at that moment, was in danger of going up in smoke. "Mount up, get out, and take the horses with you," Fargo ordered.

"Take the horses?"

"Yes, take the horses. They aren't going to stay here another ten minutes anyway, just ground-tied. I haven't got time to hobble them or rope off a corral. Leave the horses with the water wagon when you pass it. They'll have something to tie them to. When you get back, send two wagons, and make sure they're carrying stamps. Stamps, you understand? It can't be anything breakable."

"Stamps? Why do you want stamps?"

"No time to explain it," Fargo chafed. "Just go. And send those wagons back as soon as possible. And send a wagon jack, too. Don't forget the jack. And some tools. And Old Will. Oh, hell, just send Old Will and his tools."

The Trailsman waved Rogers away before he could think of anything else. What they really needed was a sudden rain, a miracle, or maybe a genie granting wishes. Or time, lots of time. Fargo wasn't at all sure that the wagons could arrive in time, but it was worth a try.

Rogers slapped his hat against his gelding's rump and thundered off with ten horses in his wake. He would never make a farmer, but he was one hell of a rider. A few years back, he had ridden for the Pony Express; that recollection lifted Fargo's spirits a bit as he retrieved his knife from its sheath.

There was nothing left to do but hack at the grass. The water wagon wouldn't be along for two hours, and the stamp-bearing wagons weren't even on their way yet.

He threw off his shirt. The sweat trickling down his chest left pale streaks in the soot. His eyes smarted so much it was hard to keep them open. His hands were raw from pulling at grass stalks that burned like rope and cut like wire. But he kept on hacking, as did the others. The Trailsman had to admit they were good men; he just hoped they were good enough.

Finally, he heard the water wagon. He wiped at the sweat on his forehead, stretched his aching back, slipped his knife back into his sheath, and walked out to the road.

The wagon was still a ways off. In the other direction, the day was dark as night except for the orange glow dancing on the horizon.

"Jameson, Campbell, Sutton, all of you, get out here. Take a break," Fargo shouted.

The men stumbled out of their newly made path through the brush just as the wagon pulled up.

"Get those oxen unhitched," Fargo roared.

The teamsters hastened to obey, but they kept glancing over their shoulders at the ten worn-out men gathered in the road.

"Jesus," Sinclair blustered. "You all look like you been trying out for one of them minstrel shows."

"Right you are," the Trailsman agreed. "Why, we've been singing and dancing and strumming all morning. Now it's your turn. You five men, take the line to the north. You, Sam"—Fargo addressed the bullwhacker—"get those oxen in the grass on the south. Have them eat it, trample it, whatever."

The oxen, like any other creatures, preferred their meals prepared. They headed right for the grass the men had spent hours cutting.

The bullwhacker cracked his whip. "You sons of Satan," he cried, "resist temptation." The whip cracked again. "Move, ye red devils of gluttony. Move or ye'll perish in brimstone where they'll roast your everlasting hides." The whip cracked a third time and the last, most obstinate steer disappeared into the tall grass.

"You men," Fargo said, "this water's for soaking, not drinking. You want to dip your hands and face in it, that's fine. Just don't spill any." The men eagerly lined up as Fargo leapt onto the wagon. They had a fire line. It was as narrow as a preacher's mind and as crooked as a drunkard's walk; with any wind, the fire would cross it without pausing to notice. But it was a start.

Jameson jumped up beside Fargo. "Looks pretty paltry to me," he commented.

The Trailsman nodded thoughtfully. Farmers were always fighting prairie fires, but they were better equipped than freighters. They had plows, scythes, hoes, shovels, and neighbors to relieve men worn out and choking on the smoke. Their plowed fields acted as natural firebreaks, and their wells were nearby.

Here the trail had swung several miles from the river.

That was a boon in the spring when the bottoms got boggy, but it was a menace now. They only had the water on the wagon. They had shovels, but prairie soil was so dense with roots that unless it was plowed or hoed first, it could break a shovel.

Fargo glanced up for a clamor down the trail. Oxen bellowed and men shouted. "What in hell?" he muttered, jumping down from the wagon. "Rogers," he muttered as he started sprinting down the road. The two wagons approaching were the prettiest sight the Trailsman had seen since leaving Sally, but he couldn't figure out how they'd arrived so soon. "How in hell did you do it?"

"Couldn't figure out what you wanted the wagons for, but figured whatever it was, you wouldn't need them tomorrow." Rogers laughed. "We were just ambling along, and the oxen were spooked and ornery, and I got to thinking. Oxen are powerful scared of fire, but they ain't none too smart. Still, they wouldn't have been ambling if they thought the fire was behind them. And I got an idea. I fixed up a torch, held it behind one fellow's ear just so he could see the flicker, and he got all excited. You know oxen, one gets hell-bent, the others follow.

"They must have run two miles flat out dragging all that tonnage behind them before they slowed again," the bullwhacker added. "You should have seen Old Will. He was up on the first wagon clinging for dear life."

"Yeah, you should've seen me," Will agreed. "I seen railroad trains move that fast, but I sure never wanted to be on one. I got no use for all this newfangled speed, but there I was rushing faster than a locomotive."

"Get those oxen turned parallel to the fire line," Fargo ordered. "And pull the wheels off the wagons. We're going to use them as plows."

"But they'll break up," Old Will complained.

"And tomorrow we'll fix them. But it's better than burning them. All of you, come out of the grass now," Fargo ordered. "Sam, get those loose oxen out of the way," he bellowed.

The Trailsman was already down on his knees helping with a wheel when Jameson came up behind him. "You mean we wasted all that time cutting grass when all we had to do was plow it?"

"Hell, no," Fargo denied. "The grass is still damp at the bottom and not easy to start. All that slash is what's going to give us one roaring backfire. Will, get as much of this hub off as you can."

Fargo stood up and slapped the dust from his knees. The smoke was getting thick. Some men coughed and sneezed as they fell to helping with the wagons, but their spirits were considerably higher than they had been earlier. That was going to count for a lot because, although Fargo wasn't sure the others realized it yet, he knew that they had just begun.

It worked. The oxen had to strain for all they were worth to get the unwheeled wagons to move, but that was for the best. The wagons balked, they caught in the sod, they tipped up clumps of it. Often the wagons stalled entirely as rooted grass mounded up in front of them; the men had to rush forward and shove aside dirt, grass, weeds, and broken saplings.

All in all, the wagons made a mess of the grass. They mashed it, milled it, and uprooted it. The first wagon was on its fourth turn when the box shifted. One side came loose in a crackling splendor of sound, a board flew up, and the men ran for cover.

"Clear that wood and keep her going," Fargo shouted; the heavy stamps were still holding the base of the box in place.

The first wagon completed five full turns before it shuddered to a halt. With one side and the back gone, the bottom planks ran askew and just wouldn't face forward. The oxen strained, but nothing moved. Fargo called for the crew to rest, but instead they gathered on the south side to cheer and whoop the other team on. These men were ready to fight.

5

They had a fire line, and it was one glorious line, almost a half-mile out from both sides of the trail and as wide as a river. But prairie fires sometimes jumped rivers.

"Campbell, Sutton, and Maxwell, grab the shovels and start spreading any loose dirt. The rest of you, grab all the loose grass and toss it west," Fargo barked.

To the west, the fire was no longer just an orange glow. It was flame, licking up the long grass and shooting into the sky. It had to be at least five miles away or the ash raining down would have included burning debris, but it looked closer.

Fargo turned to the men on the north. "Get two barrels off the wagon and start sprinkling the grass down. And for God's sake don't spill them. Don't use more water than you have to. We'll need plenty before this is over. Rogers, you swing the wagon to the other side as soon as they've got those barrels off."

Fargo gave the men their assignments. Four men to set the backfire, two on each side, one to light the burning brands, one to throw them into the loose slash. Eight men to man the fire line, the rest to guard the tallgrass behind, all armed with sopping blankets.

"With this wind, sparks are going to fly everywhere, and there's going to be fires, plenty of them," Fargo warned. "Your job is to beat them out. Whatever happens, we've got to hold this line, because if we don't, we lose everything, including us. The first one that breaks and runs, I shoot. Do you all understand?"

They all nodded, not glumly, but eagerly. They were ready for battle.

"All right," Fargo boomed. "Today you work. To-morrow you loaf. And when we get to Denver, I'll buy you three barrels of whiskey. Go!"

The men sprinted to their places. Fargo dropped his arm, and the first burning brand was tossed into the slash. The cut grass smoked and crackled. Little flames puffed up while the men ran down the line, adding fire to the fuel.

More grass caught and flames leapt up. Some tallgrass ignited and smoke billowed as the fire built and spread. Blue flame surged to orange, orange flame swelled to crimson. The wind caught it, and a column of fire soared up thirty feet, spraying brilliant sparks into the smoke-black sky. But there was no one to watch as the men whipped their sodden blankets at the fire line and the grass beyond.

Fargo, too, used a damp cloth to stop new fires. Soon his hands were blistered. His back ached from bending. His throat was raw and a cough tore at his lungs and wrenched at his gut so hard that he staggered into the tallgrass and dropped on his knees to gag up vomit and slime. As he threw back his head to gulp down fresh air, he imagined that all of his innards were coated with black tar.

There wasn't any fresh air. Still coughing, Fargo pushed himself up and stumbled back to his blanket. He picked it up and begun swinging again. His shoulders protested as if he'd been stretched on a rack. He was too dizzy to think and too tired to see anything besides flame. There wasn't anything else to see: it was as black as night. There were no more orders to give. They were past strategy. There weren't enough men left standing to bother with teamwork.

Someone shrieked, but the scream barely penetrated Fargo's consciousness. He threw back his blanket to swing it again, then hesitated when he realized the configuration of the blaze in front of him had changed because someone had fallen into the flames.

"Shit," Fargo yelled as he dropped his blanket. He grabbed the man's legs and pulled. Fargo had no idea who it was. In the orange glare, everything looked peculiar—the men, the flapping blankets, the waving wall of tallgrass, all flame and shadow, flickering light and grotesque shade. He was too damned tired, he thought. Too damned dizzy, too damned sick, and too damned sore. The man Fargo tugged moaned and turned on his side. Flame leapt off his shoulder. His shirt was on fire.

The Trailsman dropped atop of him and rolled. The earth beneath the scorched grass was hard; it hammered at Fargo's joints and rattled his already dazed senses. The man's bones gouged at him, and the rolling made him dizzier. With all of the wind knocked out of him and the man sprawled on top of him, Fargo came to rest on his back. Automatically, he slapped at the man's back and shoulders. They were mired with damp ash and muck.

"You all right?" Fargo wheezed as he pushed the man's weight off his body.

The man didn't answer, but he groaned. Fargo figured that was a good sign. He stared at the sky. There was nothing to see, no stars, no moon, no Milky Way. All had been consumed by smoke. He turned to check the man next to him, and the orange glare filled his vision; it seemed to be everywhere except directly overhead.

"You going to make it?"

"Don't know," the man whispered.

"That makes two of us," Fargo agreed as he staggered to his feet.

He groped around in the red glow until he found his damp blanket and then went back to swinging it, mindlessly, letting the rhythm drive away his pain. He didn't really notice as the glare waned. He didn't perceive that there were fewer brush fires. He just kept going until he looked around and realized there was nothing left to swat at. Exhausted, he sat down.

In the distance, the prairie fire had met the backfire. Together they made a dazzling display of crimson. Fargo shut his swollen eyes and went right on seeing flames—blue flames, yellow flames, red flames—blazing through his dreams.

When Fargo woke, it was daylight. He lay staring at the sky for several minutes before he realized it was clear. He sat up and immediately wished he'd stayed asleep.

Where he wasn't burned, he felt broken. He closed his eyes and told himself he had suffered worse, although he wasn't at all sure it was true. He felt like crawling into a hole to die. Then he remembered he was boss here. It was his job to take stock. He clenched his jaw and opened his eyes.

To the west, as far as he could see, the prairie was blackened. To the east, it hadn't fared so well either; the grass was withered, trampled on, gray with fallen ash and burned all the way to the ground in places, but for the most part they had held their fire line.

A stiff breeze had cleared away the smoke, but the air still smelled scorched. The Trailsman got up and checked on his men; not one was stirring. Although some had taken shelter under the water wagon, many still lay where they had fallen. But all of them appeared to be breathing.

A scum of ash mired the surface of the little water left in the last barrel. Beneath the scum, the water was black from having blankets immersed in it, but Fargo dipped his kerchief anyway. He washed as well as he could, then ran his hands through his hair and beard, grimacing as bits of singed frizz sprinkled down.

"Get up," he ordered, nudging first one man with his boot and then another. The men moaned and groaned. "What do you think you're doing here?" Fargo bellowed as several rolled over and tried to burrow further into the burned grass. "Do you think you can just lie around here all day? There are Indians out here. Come on. Get up."

Compared to his men, Fargo looked positively dapper. Rogers looked far worse than he had during his hay-fever attack the day before. Between the soot and the singe, his hair color was impossible to discern, and Fargo wasn't quite sure why he recognized him, but he did.

The man's face was streaked with black, and his clothes were filthy. He pushed himself up and stared at the prairie with eyes so bloodshot they were painful to behold. "We did it," he whispered hoarsely, his voice more reverent than any preacher's.

"Of course we did it," Fargo said. "Don't act so surprised. Now I'm going back to camp. You're all welcome to just loaf here until I send a wagon back for you, that's fine. But stay awake and look alive."

He turned away and started walking with his shoulders back and his lean frame straight. It took almost everything Fargo had to keep his gait steady until he was out of sight. A quarter-mile down the road, where the tallgrass rippled on both sides, he gave up the pretense. From the feel of things, a lance had surely been driven between his shoulder blades. His neck ached and his back muscles were throwing punches at his spleen.

The parts of him that weren't cramping were cracking. He had suffered sunburn, windburn, and snowburn, but his face had never felt worse, and it was all he could do to keep his hands from curling into claws. His hands were cooked, with the palms seared, the fingers parched, and the backs blistered.

But the main reason Fargo found walking so difficult was that breathing was damned near impossible. It hurt so much he didn't do it for minutes at a time, then when he did, it nearly doubled him over. His coughing had sprained every muscle in his chest. It felt worse than a half-dozen broken ribs. He'd been shot and felt better than he did as he staggered back to camp.

The prairie in late summer was a hellish place. The wind blew, but it was hot, not soothing. Flies gathered by the millions to buzz around the piles of manure left in the road. Up trail, Fargo spotted the oxen and horses accompanied by Old Will and the bullwhacker.

They were lucky, that was all there was to it, lucky that Indians hadn't swooped down while they were scattered hither and yon. Fargo couldn't afford to let his men believe that they could continue to get away with such carelessness.

"You there," Fargo shouted at Old Will, who sprawled in the shade and picked his teeth with a stem of grass. "That any way to guard livestock?"

"No, sir," Will admitted, scrambling to his feet. He was nearing sixty and he looked it, lined, stooped, heavy-set, and grizzled, but as tough as an old boot. He knew better or he wouldn't have lived so long.

It was going to take all of Fargo's talents to pull this train back into shape. Half his crew wasn't going to be good for much for a week or more. The challenge was to prevent slacking while still making them feel appreciated.

The only way Fargo knew how to do that was to set a good example. He couldn't drive men already on the edge, but maybe he could inspire them. Fargo found and mounted his Ovaro.

"Wouldn't have liked it at all if you'd let the Indians ride off with my horse," he commented mildly. "Wouldn't be real happy if you lost these critters, either," he added, pointing to the oxen strung out every which way, some grazing and some just sunning themselves. "So keep your weapons to the fore and start herding them in. I'm sending a wagon back for the other men. The fire's out."

Fargo spurred the Ovaro and left a cloud of dust behind. As he rode, he pressed his fist to his chest. Talking had used up his supply of air, and the new air he'd taken in didn't seem to want to fit.

He reined up, vaulted off his horse, and sprinted for the grass, where he coughed, choking up gray mucus until he felt he'd turned himself inside out. Although he felt empty, Fargo knew he was filled with gray sludge and he would be for days, maybe weeks.

He rose, stumbled to the Ovaro, and clung to the saddle horn just to stay upright. His burned hands cringed, his knees were shaky, and his head whirled. He wasn't sure he would ever be able to mount.

Somehow he managed to straddle his horse while black dots swam before his eyes, threatening to swamp what little consciousness he had left. He let the Ovaro walk, hoping it would give him time to revive before he got back to camp.

Amos was ahead of him on the trail, Amos on a sturdy dun, Amos who never rode a horse. A lot of bullwhackers didn't, since they spent their lives walking from Council Bluffs to Santa Fe, from Missouri to Oregon, from Leavenworth to Denver. What use did they have for a horse?

Fargo straightened and tried to get his head to clear while anxiety pressed on his chest from front and back, making it doubly difficult to breathe.

"Something's wrong," he said flatly as Amos drew abreast.

Winfield nodded. "It's Sally."

"Sally?" Fargo repeated. "What the hell does she have to do with anything? For God's sake Amos, if you've got something to confess about Sally don't do it now."

Amos spat as he wheeled his horse around. "You'll find out soon enough. And damn you, Skye Fargo, I hope she gives you more trouble than you can handle. You deserve it."

Fargo stared after Winfield's back. He had never heard the huge man swear before, and all because of something about Sally. How much trouble could the woman cause Fargo when he was way out here, anyway? And why would Amos have ridden forward with such a strange message?

Camp seemed serene. The wagons were pulled into a circle, but several men stood outside the perimeter to guard the oxen that grazed outside the enclosure. The sentries noted Fargo's arrival, but they turned back almost immediately to keep their eyes on the range.

Fargo turned his horse over to a guard. "Tend to him for me, will you?" he asked.

He went and washed again, splashing water in his

face, pouring it over his head and dousing his torso with it, hoping it would perk him up. It didn't. He donned fresh clothes anyway and looked for Amos. Fargo found Winfield crouched over, fiddling with the chains that connected two wagons. He straightened upon hearing Fargo's step.

"Look, Amos, whatever it was I said, I'm sorry. We'll talk about it later. But right now I've got to get a wagon down to collect the men from the fire detail. And it looks like we're going to have to lay over a few days for repairs. I thought maybe we could move the train down to the river, where there's plenty of water and a little shade. What do you think?"

Winfield eyed Fargo sullenly, but Fargo had no wind left, none whatsoever, so he had no choice except to wait to make amends with his old friend.

"I can handle those things," Amos said. "But first I got something for you to handle." With fists clenched at his sides, the huge man towered over Fargo.

Deciding that this was surely not his day, Fargo waited for the blow, but Winfield spun instead. He jumped over the chains and leaned into the wagon. "Get over here," he thundered.

Dazed, the Trailsman watched as Winfield jerked back from the wagon, pulling Sally with him.

"What in hell?" Fargo breathed.

"Don't ask me," Winfield snapped. "I just found her here. I didn't put her here."

"Then who?"

"Chatham, from what she says. But he's gone, slunk off into the night like a coyote. Couldn't find hide nor hair of him this morning." Amos released Sally's wrist and started walking away.

Chatham? He was a small, skinny redhead, an experienced bullwhacker. Fargo had been glad to find him for the crew. This didn't seem like something Chatham would do, but the world was full of things that didn't add up.

"Wait," Fargo croaked.

"Oh, no. She's your problem now, not mine. No

matter what you think, she never was mine, and I sure as hell ain't taking her now. I got more important things to tend to."

"And I don't?" Fargo protested, but Winfield was gone. He had stalked right off in midsentence, while Sally cowered, tears running down her flushed cheeks.

Greasy at the roots, her tied-back hair fell in limp, dust-laden tangles across her shoulders. Dirty and sweaty, she wore a plain gray cotton dress that was layered with dust and stained everywhere. With both hands she clutched a shabby carpetbag heavy enough to make her lean to the side it weighted down. A black smudge tipped her nose.

"You look terrible," Fargo observed.

"You wouldn't look so wonderful yourself if you'd been hiding in a wagon for nearly a week."

"I don't look so wonderful as it is," he countered. "But why, Sally? Why are you here?"

She took a deep breath and fell into a siege of weeping. "Oh, Skye, I'm sorry. I just didn't think, really I didn't. But hiding on your train seemed like such a good idea at the time, since I couldn't stay at Lilabeth's. She was so angry about me spending the whole week with you. And she wanted money, and I couldn't give her my money, since you took it away from me before you left.

"I guess I understand you demanding my share of the money, Skye, since I made it by knocking you out and all, but I kind of figured you owed me something, and I knew Chatham pretty well, and . . . and . . ." Sally choked on a long, wheezy gasp. "Please, Skye, please," she squeaked. "You're not really angry, are you?"

It all sounded so familiar—Sally gibbering and her voice rising into shrill soprano. Fargo felt much the same as he had when he'd come awake so abruptly in his hotel room—dizzy, light-headed, nauseated. But he had thought he'd gotten Sally all squared away in those last minutes when she had lain there naked, needling him to admit it had all been worth it. He had been so warm, satiated, and content right then that he had almost been fool enough to admit it had been worth it.

But, instead, he had gotten a mite irritated with her self-satisfied, "cat who ate the cream and then some" smile, and therefore demanded the money. At the time it had seemed to serve her right. He had even congratulated himself. Skye Fargo was a man who knew how to handle women. Remembering it all, he felt like laughing, but he was afraid that he would cough his guts out.

"What am I supposed to do with you?" Fargo wondered.

"Well, I did have an idea," she ventured.

"An idea?" Fargo echoed. He hadn't expected an answer. And he certainly didn't want one from Sally. It showed on his face.

"I mean, I didn't just come along without any thought as to what I'd do and, well, there was . . ." Sally glanced up at Fargo cautiously, then ducked her head back down. "Never mind," she told him. "I knew you wouldn't want to help. I've said I was sorry till I was blue in the face, but you don't listen even when I admit I was wrong although all I ever wanted to do was get away from Lilabeth. And that's why, when Webster offered that money, I just couldn't find it in myself to turn it down, except you took it from me, and I didn't know what to do because nobody cares, nobody ever cares that Lilabeth near robs her girls blind and never gives them a night off, come hell or Sunday, and charges a fortune in rent just for a bed, and—"

"Enough," Fargo broke in, wishing he'd found her before the fire. The woman was a phenomenon; she didn't need air. "What's your idea? And you'd better make it short because I've got work to do."

"I want to get married."

"Married?" Fargo coughed on the word, and his lungs squeezed painfully. He clutched at his chest and stumbled over to the wagon.

"You don't have to act that way," Sally cried. "I just said I wanted to get married. I didn't say it had to be to you, and there's nothing wrong with me. I can cook and clean if I have to, and I'm willing to work, and I know how to keep chickens, and I suppose I can learn how to milk a cow, and I'd bet there's plenty of men who would be pleased to have me for—"

"Why?"

"Why?" Sally shrieked. "Why, Skye Fargo, you are so mean. How can you say that when there are hardly any women in Colorado at all, and everyone says the men there will marry most anyone who still has some teeth? I know what I've been, but I'm not really so bad, and I can't see how you can say that after you and me, and me and you, well . . ." Sally finished in a torrent of tears that could have put out the prairie fire.

"For God's sake, Sally. I was only trying to ask why you wanted to get married and do all that tedious farmwork." Fargo took too deep a breath and the lower parts of his lungs seemed to tear away from their moorings. "Jesus," he whispered, staggering sideways. The coughing exploded out of him, wrenching at his chest, and he dropped onto his hands and knees.

"Dear God," Sally cried. "You're sick. Why didn't you say something? Here, let me help you." Sally dropped down on her knees beside him and reached out with tentative fingers to touch his cheek. "You're clammy, but not feverish. Is it broken ribs? Is that it?"

"Go away," Fargo breathed out, fairly sure that he'd never breathe in again.

"I can't. I can't leave you like this."

"I've got to get away," Fargo rasped. "Tell Amos. Tell him I'm scouting. By the river. Nothing else."

"But Skye—"

"Please," he hissed.

Sally bounded up and ran off while Fargo choked up more mucus. Using the wagon wheel, he managed to get back on his feet.

6

Because people traveling the trail often came here, a path ran along the river, wending between shrubby chokecherries and around tangled clumps of aster just beginning to bloom. The white flowers with their scruffy gold centers looked like scraggly daisies stretching for the sun, a sun that was suffocatingly hot. Cottonwoods beside the Little Blue offered shade, although they weren't very big, since prairie fires wiped them out on a fairly regular basis.

Fargo found a grassy clearing beneath a tree and threw his bedroll down. Immediately, a swarm of green midges rose up from the grass while hoppers sailed off in all directions. Within seconds, a host of fat black flies hummed over to check him out. Frowning, he considered moving to less inhospitable ground.

Farther afield, a stand of bur oak shaded the path, but the things were prickly. Closer to him, Sally scampered up the path, looking pleased with herself. Fargo hadn't wanted her to come, but she had pestered like a bratty six-year-old, threatening to tell Amos on him if he wouldn't bring her along.

It hadn't taken Sally five minutes to figure out that she could take advantage of Fargo's reluctance to have his men know that he wasn't feeling up to snuff. So here he was in Indian country, not in any condition to take care of himself, let alone a woman, while she darted around and admired the weeds as if she were tripping through a flower garden.

Deciding that he wasn't likely to find a better place in spite of these hungry natives, Fargo spread his bedroll, but no matter how much he fussed with the blankets, he couldn't seem to get comfortable. The heat made him damp and the dampness made his shirt stick to his scorched back. He threw his shirt off, so the flies gathered to investigate his burns.

He stretched out flat on his back, but it felt like he'd landed in a vat of lye. He turned on his stomach, but the pressure on his lungs made it impossible to breathe. He tried rolling onto his side and decided he was too sore to lie down at all. When he leaned against the tree, the bark clawed at his abused back. So he sat square in the middle of his bedroll, wishing he was a horse because horses slept just fine on their feet.

Not that Fargo planned on sleeping, not with Sally along, but he felt he deserved a little rest. He glanced over his shoulder to check on the woman, but she wasn't where she was supposed to be.

"Dammit, I told you to stay on this side of the path. And keep away from there," he shouted as she skipped over to embrace a stand of blue vervain. Even from here, he could practically hear the bees buzzing around the riot of tiny violet flowers tipping those long leafy stalks. "You're going to get stung," he warned.

"Don't worry," she called back. "Bees don't seem to like me much."

"Damn, and I never thought of bees as intelligent before." Fargo turned back to watch the Little Blue roll by.

It was a hot, lazy kind of day, good for fishing and loafing, but Fargo wasn't in any mood to enjoy it. He wasn't just sore, he was on edge. He had suffered one three-day delay and he hadn't thought it mattered, but now there was this delay, which endangered his men and his train.

Fargo was tired of suspecting his own men. The truth was, he did trust his men, even if he wasn't sure it was wise. Besides, he couldn't find it in himself to distrust Amos anymore, and although "trust" wasn't exactly his attitude toward Sally, he couldn't really believe she was capable of lying. Lies required finesse, and Sally couldn't keep a story straight if she was reading it aloud.

Fargo could only conclude that Webster and McCormick really had paid Sally an outrageous sum to delay him for no apparent reason. And if they had done that, they may well have set the trail fire, which meant that it was time to scout ahead to see just what else Webster and McCormick were up to.

But if he was wrong?

If someone from his own train had set that fire, then leaving wasn't a very good idea. But Fargo was going to go anyway, because in the end, a man had to rely on his instincts, and his instincts told him to trust his men and Amos and even Sally—to a degree.

The best thing about laying all the blame on Webster and McCormick was that he hadn't liked them at all. Webster was an oily sort with slicked-back hair and a waxed mustache, a dandy who obviously thought he was a striking gent, although his face was too lean and his smile was too patent.

McCormick, an ordinary sort with brown hair, brown eyes, and an average build, was a glad-hander with sweaty palms. Even though he needn't have stood out in a crowd, McCormick's tendency to smile too much and to slap everyone on the back with jolly regularity made him the type of man that Fargo suspected and avoided.

Both were bootlickers who wanted their boots licked in return. When Fargo hadn't bothered, they had quickly revealed themselves as the puffed-up, insolent sons of bitches they really were. Webster had insisted that in spite of his fame as a tracker, Skye Fargo was essentially a man of unsavory character, a womanizer, and a whiskey-drinker, while McCormick had maintained that the Trailsman was only interested in horning in on their profits, a ridiculous notion, since all Fargo had requested in return for combining their trains was a hundred-dollar bonus for Amos.

The Trailsman would be glad to blame all his problems on Webster and McCormick, but unfortunately not even fools plagued relative strangers for no reason. So there had to be a reason. Fargo only wished he could think of one. But it didn't matter. He had made his decision. He was going after them.

Now he had to decide whether to do so as soon as he was feeling up to it, which he had already decided would have to be tomorrow, or whether he should wait until the train was back on the road and past the burn-out. Fargo could feel the tightness in his chest and the coughing impulse scratching at his throat, but he didn't have time for it. He was going to feel better by tomorrow even if he had to learn to sleep standing up.

Two thousand dollars and a prairie fire would indicate that there was a substantial motive for delaying Fargo and his caravan. But how substantial? Were they going to try something else? What would they try? When? Why? "Damn," Fargo muttered, because he had no idea.

"Skye?"

"What?" he chafed, glancing up to find Sally hovering over him.

"Do you think it would be all right if I washed up here?"

"From the looks of you, it might not be a bad idea at all."

"You don't have to be mean about it," she complained.

"And you didn't have to come," he reminded her.

"Well, thanks," she huffed, flouncing off.

"Anytime," Fargo called after her, knowing that sooner or later he was also going to have to deal with the problem of Sally. It was not a good idea to have a whore along on a train with thirty-six men who were supposed to be minding business, not pleasure.

The woman had no modesty. "What are you doing?" Fargo asked as she shed her clothes. "You said you were going to wash, not swim."

"Does it matter?"

Fargo scanned the banks, the grassy inlet, the rip-

71

pling water, the sandy shoal. If Indians did arrive unexpectedly, they'd have the same idea of what to do with her whether she was dressed or naked. "I suppose not," he admitted.

There were women as lithe and muscular as cats, and women with faces as delicate as porcelain dolls, exotic women, graceful women, elegant women. Sally wasn't any of those, but for her type, she was as near perfect as they came. She was cute with an almost puppy-dog appeal. Her round brown eyes were rimmed by dark spiky lashes. Her pouty lips were bright with color.

She had dimples when she smiled. She was just plump enough to be extra cuddly with cushioning across her breasts, and skin as soft as a baby's bottom, and a belly that curved right into a man's hand.

Oblivious to the grass tickling her bare ass, Sally knelt over the ratty carpetbag she had insisted they bring along. Fargo tried to ignore her, but she even had two tiny dimples on her bottom.

"Don't go out too far," he warned.

Sally turned her head toward him and nodded while pulling her dirty curls back. Her hair fell across her hips, covering her round little rump, and Fargo turned his thoughts back to Webster and McCormick.

Maybe they had some personal grudge against him, he mused. They certainly hadn't treated him with any courtesy.

He glanced up to see that Sally had followed his advice for once. She could have gone out a little farther than she had. The water barely reached her thighs, and sunlight glistened off her wet breasts and belly. With determination, Fargo forced his thoughts back to Webster.

"You just stay away from our train," Webster had said. So maybe it was something about the train itself that he didn't want Fargo delving into. Contraband? Whiskey maybe?

But that would be stupid. Whiskey was the one thing the folks in Denver never risked going without.

They kept huge stocks at hand. If Denver was shut off for an entire year, it wouldn't run short of whiskey, and thus the price of whiskey seldom fluctuated. Hazarding an Indian uprising to supply whiskey wouldn't pay any more than delivering it later.

Sally soaped her breasts languidly. She was putting on quite a show, although she really didn't need to. She lifted them one at a time to wash underneath, then paused to circle her nipples with her fingertips as if playing with herself. Her breasts were large and well-rounded, with nipples jutting upward. Fargo shifted his gaze to the chokecherries lining the path and his thoughts to his problems.

So what could Webster and McCormick be carrying on their train that they didn't want anyone to see? Explosives, maybe? Hell, even if they planned on blowing up the governor, it would be easy to explain hauling explosives to a mining territory. Guns? No, it couldn't be. There definitely was nothing wrong with guns. Those who complained about the abundance of guns in the West were always from the East.

No matter how hard he tried, Fargo couldn't think of anything that was worth hiding on a train. Nothing was contraband in the Colorado Territory. Embarrassing maybe, and from what he'd seen of Webster and McCormick, they were the kind of men who worried more about looking good than being good. But Fargo doubted they would pay two thousand dollars to avoid embarrassment.

So what were they up to? A Wells Fargo heist? Mail fraud? A bank robbery? The hard cases they had hired sure looked up to that sort of thing. But if so, why not wait until the Indians had calmed down and the trail wasn't crawling with military escorts?

Indians. Fargo felt his blood surge. It was the best explanation he had come upon so far. Maybe they were trafficking with the Indians. In that case, whiskey, explosives, guns, any one of those things would ruin a man's good reputation forever, and they would probably get him lynched, besides.

The Trailsman stretched. Sally was leaning back to rinse her hair out, and her breasts surged impossibly high above the water. They were as large as halved muskmelons even when she was flat on her back.

Fargo knew that she had to be kneeling under the water with her thighs spread wide to keep her balance. All he had to do was shed his trousers and walk over there. Sally wouldn't have been showing off so much if that wasn't what she wanted.

"Oh, no, you don't," he said aloud. "Now, where was I? Indians. That's it. They're trafficking with Indians. But, hell, that doesn't make any sense either."

The Indians were warring because they were starving. The buffalo were vanishing and they had nothing to trade. Arapaho men were selling their wives for plugs of tobacco. Buffalo hides, buckskin, and pelts were scarce now, so all the Indians had to trade were women and horses. Although Fargo suspected that, given a choice, most men, white or red, would prefer to relinquish their wives before their horses, it was a moot point among the Indians. Since so many of their horses were stolen, the animals weren't real negotiable. So Fargo was back with Webster and McCormick after him for no reason.

He sighed, inhaled, and coughed repeatedly. Grasping the tree, he staggered to his feet, hoping a new position would relieve the spasms in his chest.

"Skye, are you all right?" Sally called.

"I'm fine," he rasped, turning away. Every time he went into Sally, he came out with more trouble than he'd bargained for. He wasn't going to do it again, but on the other hand, just the thought of it took the edge off of his aches and pains.

It was uncommonly hot. Grass, blue vervain, chokecherries, cottonwood, bur oak, asters, sunflowers, and black-eyed Susans sat still as death while insects hummed noisily, flitting from flower to flower. No wind, no breeze, just heavy, sultry heat. Why now? he wondered. Why not yesterday when the prairie fire would have died of boredom under such conditions?

Fargo was tired, he felt frustrated and he hurt a lot more than he cared to admit, even to himself. He tensed as he felt Sally move behind him.

"Dear God, you're a mess," she blurted.

Fargo whirled. "You're dressed," he said, feeling absurdly disappointed.

Sally held a brush in one hand and tilted her head to finish brushing a stroke through the wet hair streaming across her breast. She was clothed from head to foot, although bare toes peeked from beneath the hem of her yellow cotton dress.

"A mess? What in hell does that mean?" Fargo asked belatedly.

"You've got little blisters all over your back. And now, look at you. Here you are without a shirt, exposing the worst sunburn I ever did see, and you don't seem to care at all."

"It's not a sunburn."

Sally's eyes grew wide. "You got that from the fire?"

"What do you know about the fire?" Fargo demanded.

"Well, most everything, I guess. I heard you shouting orders and then everybody else started shouting. And then you ordered a wagon unloaded to haul water. And then somebody came and got two more wagons. And then Amos ordered another two wagons emptied because he thought you might need them up at the fire to ferry back hurt men and the like. And that's when Chatham came and told me I was on my own because we were sure as hell going to get caught, what with everybody unloading wagons right and left. And he was right, because Amos found me, which I guess was for the best, because I don't know what would have happened without Chatham to bring food and water and signal when the coast was clear."

"Signal when the coast was clear?"

"Why, sure. A body can't survive in a hot, airless wagon without ever getting out."

"You mean you've been wandering around my camp, right under my nose? Who else knew?"

Sally blushed scarlet and her jaw trembled. "Please, Skye, don't ask me any more questions. I can't tell you. Chatham betrayed me, but the others . . ."

"What others?"

"Oh, please, no. I can't," she gasped, turning her tears on full force.

"Amos?"

"No, not Amos. I swear. Amos wouldn't. You know that. I told you that before. He and me, we aren't—"

"Then who?" Fargo gritted.

"I can't," Sally whimpered, shaking her head. "I can't tell you, Skye."

Fargo grasped her forearm. "You had better tell me."

She clamped her eyes shut and trembled all over. "I can't," she insisted.

"Sally." Fargo squeezed her forearm.

She flinched and clamped her jaw tight.

"Dammit," Fargo cursed, thrusting her arm away and stomping off. He wheeled back to face her. "What am I supposed to do with you? Someone tries to burn my whole damned train, and you're keeping secrets."

"What?" she whispered.

"Somebody set that fire. Surely you overheard that, too. Unless you knew about it beforehand."

Sally's wide eyes popped open. "Oh, God, no. I wouldn't, I didn't, I swear," she squeaked. "I swear."

Dropping onto Fargo's bedroll, Sally sat with her hands covering her face while she rocked back and forth. She sobbed, gasping in spurts of air and letting them build in her chest.

"Goddammit, don't screech at me," Fargo exploded. "Whatever you do, just don't start screeching. I can't take it. You make sounds only owls should make."

"Ohhhh," Sally sobbed, seemingly unable to help it. She pulled her knees up, wrapping her arms around her legs and burying her face in her dress. Her shoulders heaved.

"For God's sake, Sally, cut it out. I didn't kill you last time, and I suppose I won't this time. But you are wearing seriously on my patience." The Trailsman sat down beside her, but he wasn't sure how to get her attention.

She muffled her sobs against her skirt and shivered like a quaky.

He reached over and touched her hair. "Sally, you've got to tell me. I've got to know what the men on my train are up to."

"Nothing," she gasped. "I swear they haven't done anything."

"Don't you think I should be the judge of that? Sally, just tell me what you know."

She raised her head tentatively and glanced at Fargo. It didn't seem fair to him. She was the one who had drugged him and stolen away on his train, and yet she made him feel guilty.

"I don't know anything," she said. "I didn't have anything to do with the fire and I don't even know the men on your train, except for you and Amos and maybe some of the others, but . . . Skye, I don't even know who's on your train."

"Sally, you said there were others."

"Oh, God, I always talk too much."

Fargo couldn't believe she was doing it to him again. Every time Sally did something audacious, she wept and whimpered until he felt like the hangman. "Dammit, Sally. I'm being reasonable here. I'm not asking too much."

"Oh, Skye, I know," she cried, burying her face back in her dress. "But I can't, I can't, I just can't," she chanted. "Please, Skye, I'm sorry. Really I am. But I didn't have anything to do with that fire. I wouldn't do that to you. And your back, it looks so terrible. And you won't let me help you. Oh, Skye, did you have to get so close?"

"So close to what? Do you mean the fire? Oh, no, of course not," he denied angrily. "Why, we could have just gone downtown and called on the hook-and-ladder company, and they would have brought their big white horses and their pump engines and their hoses and drowned that fire in an instant. But we preferred to do it the hard way. It was more fun. What do you think, Sally? That fire was serious business, and yet you—"

In his anger, Fargo had forgotten to breathe carefully, and he gagged on the mounting constriction in his throat. "Oh, damn," he cursed, lurching to his feet.

He bounded over to the bushes on bare feet and dutifully knelt to choke up mucus. It wasn't as bad as it had been, but it didn't go away any easier. He coughed, wheezed, coughed again, repeatedly, until finally he could sit back on his heels feeling drained.

"Let me help you," Sally pleaded.

"Get lost!"

"But I want to help you."

"You mean you're going to talk?" he asked gruffly, his voice hoarse. "Well, hell, I should have tried choking to death earlier."

Fargo stood and walked past Sally. Grass and weeds poked at his bare feet, making him tread more gingerly on his way back to his bedroll. When he'd been sprinting into the bushes, he hadn't even noticed the prickly footing.

"Skye, I still can't talk, but maybe this will help." Sally thrust a jar in front of him.

"What is it?"

"It's for your back."

"Oh, no, you don't. There's a saying about trusting folks at your back."

"There is?"

"There sure is. Trust a stranger at your back and he's likely to blow it clear through to your front."

"You're calling me a stranger?" she whispered.

Fargo sat back down and glowered at her. "I could think of worse things to call you, and believe me, I have. What would you call yourself? A friend? No, Sally, you're no friend of mine. Goddammit," he snapped, leaning forward. "Now I've got stickers between my toes."

7

Sally took a long unsteady breath.

"Dammit, woman, don't cry," Fargo commanded. "You don't have my permission to cry unless I beat you."

She squeezed her eyes shut, screwed up her face, and clamped down on her bottom lip with her teeth, but to Fargo's amazement, she didn't cry. She trembled and huffed as if she had been running in a horse race without a horse, but she still didn't cry.

"You'd better sit down before you fall down," Fargo suggested.

Sally sat obediently, with her hands folded in her lap and her eyes cast down like a child sent to the corner. She didn't say a word. A quiet Sally made Fargo feel more guilty than his temper had. He glanced at the jar in her skirts. "You really think that stuff will help?"

She was up and at his back before he could say another word. And she was wary enough to make him feel like an ogre. Her fingers fluttered like butterflies, dabbing on the cream.

"I don't break so easy. You can just spread that goop on."

Her fingers worked more surely, but remained gentle. Fargo crossed his arms and leaned against his knees; his chest felt better and there was a breeze starting—a warm breeze, to be sure, but one that chased the stillness away. As Sally worked the cream in, her fingers stroked to places Fargo knew weren't burnt. Pressing into his backbone, they eased out the tension and soothed away the brittleness.

"You ever fire a rifle?" Fargo asked.

"Yes," she whispered.

"You think you could handle a Henry?"

"The sixteen-shooter?" She almost sounded excited.

Fargo twisted around and eyed her dubiously. "Have you got another surprise for me? An army waiting out there or something?"

Sally's face collapsed.

Fargo laid his fingers on her lips. "No, don't cry. Truth is, I guess I can appreciate your loyalty, even as misbegotten as it is." He slipped his fingers under Sally's chin and tilted her face up, caressing her jaw with his thumb. "But I want you to think on one thing: I'm in charge of the train, and I really believe it would be a lot safer for everyone involved if I knew more."

"Oh, Skye, I'm sure you'll find out soon enough," she whispered, her voice husky with emotion, but no longer shrill with hysteria. "But I can't. They'd think I did it for you."

"Is there something wrong with doing it for me?"

"Well, you know. For sex. They'd think I put that first. Before them. Before any promises I've made. So many folks seem to think a woman will betray anything or anyone for a lover."

"For sex? I didn't even think of that. I guess it wouldn't work, would it?"

Sally stared at him, her eyes luminous, her lips parted, and her breath coming too fast.

Fargo had been teasing, but he had never seen yearning glow so transparently in a woman's eyes. Fascinated, he leaned forward and pressed his lips over hers.

Breath soughed from her, warm on his tongue. She fell against him, quivering all over as he slipped his arms around her. He pressed his advantage, pushing her down, and Sally dropped onto her back.

"Please, Skye, I can't," she pleaded.

"Sure you can," he assured her, locking his lips over hers to prevent further protest. He found the hem of her gown with one hand while still clasping Sally tightly in his embrace. His fingers glided around her ankle and up the back of her calf while his lips slid along her jaw to nuzzle at the back of her ear.

"I can't," she protested.

Fargo eased his hand up. Her thighs parted. Sally didn't have a stitch on beneath her dress. His knuckles grazed her dampness, and she bore down, spreading her legs wide.

The woman unfurled like a flower opening for the sun. Sensing his power, Fargo poised his hand right there, where he could feel her dew, and Sally pressed forward, pursuing the touch he kept just out of reach, while her whole body quivered with agitation.

"Please, Skye, don't make me do this," she begged shakily. "Try to understand. I want to get married and be an honest woman. If I'd betray my friends for you . . ."

"I take it you're hoping to marry one of the friends you're not telling me about."

Sally's eyes flew open. "Oh, no," she objected. "It's nothing like that." Sally's cheeks flushed crimson and perspiration moistened the skin above her lip. She was hot, as hot as he had ever seen a woman.

Fargo wasn't feeling particularly cool himself. Just the smell of her in the sultry afternoon heat made him sweat.

The fire mounted in his own loins, but he resisted that urgent message. Sally's desperate lust astounded him. He stretched out a finger experimentally and marveled as she shuddered. With only a fingertip in her pulsing flesh, he pressed his lips to her throat, amused by the way she tried to squirm down over his hand.

"Oh, God, Skye. I don't want to hurt my friends. And I've got to get married. My mama's been so sick, and I can't go home to her until I've quit being a whore, but I thought I could be good. I meant to be a faithful wife, and now look at me. What am I doing, Skye?"

She was trying to impale herself on Fargo's finger, that's what she was doing. He pulled his hand out from under her skirt and grabbed his belt buckle, while Sally rolled onto her side and pressed herself against his thigh, her hips undulating.

"Dear God, I want you," she breathed as her hand moved under Fargo's to help him with his pants. "I don't deserve a husband. Although I never meant to ask for much. I didn't expect him to be faithful. I thought it would be all right if he could have other women, thought he wouldn't be so bothered by what I've been."

Fargo shoved his pants down and Sally grasped his shaft. "I meant to let him come and go as he pleased," she continued. "I didn't even expect him to support me." Sally's voice, hushed and breathy, rose and fell with her unsteady respiration. "I just wanted a home. A little respectability. Some babies. I don't mind working. Clerking in a store. Or selling eggs. Or anything."

Sally's finger's clutched at Fargo's erection as she tugged her skirt up. "Dear God, I thought I could be true!"

"Sally, you're not even married yet," Fargo reminded.

"But I promised my friends," she whimpered. "I'm just no good. I never have been. I can't pretend. And you know what kind of man is going to marry me. He'll be ugly, he'll drink too much, and he'll be mean sometimes. If I can't stay true to friends that have always been good to me, how am I going to be true to him? And I so wanted to please my mama. I wanted to be married for her."

Sally buried her face against Fargo's shoulder and her hand tugged on his shaft. Her thumb circled the tip of his erection, tantalizing him with his own sticky moisture, and the tension mounted in his groin, knotting up into his belly and pulling at his thighs. Fargo knew that all he had to do to get Sally to quit her incessant whining was release her from her bargain, but he wasn't going to do it. He wasn't about to be manipulated that way. Besides, he really needed to know who her friends were. It was his business, fair or unfair.

"Dammit, Sally," he said, pushing her away from him, and sitting up, "that's the stupidest reason I've ever heard for getting married. If you want to please your mother, send her a box of candy. Now, dry your eyes and get out of this," he ordered, fingering the yellow cotton of her bodice and the breast beneath it. "I want to feel your teats pressed against me. As for your friends, I'm not planning on murdering them. If, after I talk to them, I don't think they had anything to do with the prairie fire, I'll likely just dock their pay."

"You can't do that."

"I can do what I have to. Your blathering won't stop me. For God's sake, Sally, my men had no right to bring a woman along. Surely even you can see that. So quit trying to weasel out of your deal."

"Is that what I'm doing?" Sally lay on her back gazing up at Fargo with dazed eyes. Her skirts were bunched around her thighs.

"Yes," he answered, grasping a thigh with one hand. His fingers poked under the yellow cotton to tease the soft inner flesh at the top of her leg, and she inhaled sharply. Tossing her skirts higher, he glanced down at his own hand. He stretched his fingers and she gasped again. "Well, do we have a deal?" he asked gruffly.

"Oh, please, Skye. Please, don't make me. It doesn't matter anyway. You'll find out soon enough. And they'll hate me if I tell you. They already know how I feel, and they'll know what I've done."

"So they know you pretty well, huh? This well?" he asked, sliding his index finger into her.

"No," Sally groaned, twisting into his grasp. "Skye, you don't understand."

"So why don't you tell me."

Sally studied his face, then lowered her eyes slowly, letting her gaze linger on his chest, his tight muscles, his lean torso, until finally she was staring directly at his erect shaft. "I will," she sighed.

"Now!"

"No, not now," she begged. "You'll get upset. You'll get mad. You'll leave."

"You think I'll leave?" He laughed. "Well, maybe I will," he told her, knowing that he was lying, but figuring that he was better at it than she was. "But I'm going to leave sooner if you don't tell me," he warned. "You've got two seconds to give me those names."

Her thighs were spread wide and her muscles pulsed against his finger. She was slick and hot and ready.

Fargo ached to get past this foolishness, but she had started it, he hadn't. "Who?" he demanded.

"After," she moaned, writhing against his hand. "I'll tell you after."

"You'll tell me now."

"No, dammit. You're not being fair. I haven't lied to you. And I won't. But I can't because you won't . . . Oh, Skye, it's such a long story."

Sally's hips came off the bedroll as she whipped sideways and grasped Fargo's pelvis. Before he could stop her, she rolled into a ball, pressing her face to his lap. Fargo half-expected her to bite him, but her mouth merely closed over his shaft.

"Oh, shit," he murmured as Sally turned tables on him. The tip of her tongue probed and twisted at the top of his organ, giving him the strangest feeling that she was thrusting into him. Her lips slipped farther down, taking more of him in than he would have thought possible, as she embraced him with a tongue as lithe and treacherous as a snake's.

Sally lathed him with her tongue until he fell back onto his elbows and drove himself into her mouth. She followed him down, her tongue still twirling and twisting. Then, sucking in her cheeks, she pulled back, nearly taking him with her. Sally's lips dragged free, releasing Fargo with a loud smack.

"After," she whispered.

"Oh, hell," he groaned. His breathing was shaky, but Fargo had long since forgotten his lungs, his aches, his pains, his ravaged back. All his sensations were centered on his throbbing shaft. "All right," he agreed while clutching her skirt in his fist. "But take this damned thing off first."

Sally offered him a tremulous smile. "Thank you," she murmured, blowing him a kiss through her swollen red lips as she fumbled with the buttons high on the back of her dress. Her cheeks were bright, her eyes were lustrous, and she looked radiant.

Fargo eyed her quizzically. He didn't know how much he had won or lost in their game, but he doubted that anyone ever really knew the score when playing with the opposite sex. But Sally looked so serene. Maybe he was missing something.

"You need help?" he asked.

"I can handle it." She was already tugging her dress over her head.

Fargo certainly didn't want to get the question of some pleasure all mixed up with the business of who her friends were, but he couldn't help but wonder whether Sally thought the issue was resolved. Because it wasn't. In all good conscience as a wagon master, Fargo had to pursue it.

But it could wait, he decided as her breasts bounced free of the yellow cotton. He reached out and cupped them in his hands, pushing her back as he fondled them. He was atop her almost immediately, burying himself to the hilt between her fleshy thighs. He wanted it to be quick and hard and sweaty. As far as Fargo was concerned, he had waited long enough.

Sally didn't seem to mind. She strained against him, pulling her knees up high and grasping at his buttocks, while Fargo slammed into her furiously. He felt good again, with his pain banished and his energy restored. And Sally's muscles clamored for him, pulsing wildly as she groaned with frenzy.

Arching into him and pressing with all her might, she vibrated from head to toe. She pressed against Fargo as if she could fuse them together. Her body was rigid, but quivering, inside and out. She was hot and wet, but she sizzled like lightning ready to strike.

Tension soared high in Fargo, screaming for release.

His world narrowed to a single dark tunnel. Pulsing and demanding, it lured him on, carrying him to the edge of awareness where he was only vaguely conscious of Sally, sweat-soaked and slick beneath him. His muscles labored with need and urgency, driving him into her.

Sally surrounded him, clutching at his sides with her legs while her hands grappled for his ass, trying to make him stay in. He lunged harder, and she renewed her efforts. She flung her arms around his neck and wrapped her legs around his middle.

Her full breasts molded to him like warm wax as her soft, slippery belly seemed to ooze right into him. She swamped Fargo with her moist, sticky heat. While he strove to ram himself into her hot throbbing center, she seemed to be trying to glue them together. Her arms tightened around his neck like a noose.

His reaction was instantaneous. He bore down on her, pushing her shoulders back, and her arms loosened. But her legs gripped fiercely. Desperate to stay close, Sally jerked into him, squeezing him with her thighs and jamming her pelvis down. His body retaliated, pumping her full of liquid heat while filling him with release.

Sally screamed and writhed. Her interior muscles thundered and she pitched into manic gyrations. Fargo rode it out. He ached and felt weary, but blissfully content, with all of his sharp-edged pains lost in a haze and all of his worries forgotten, for the moment.

Fargo slipped off Sally, but stayed close. She made a nice pillow, and leaning on her took some of the pressure off his work-sore shoulder.

"I considered sending you back to Leavenworth," he told her. "But it wouldn't be safe without an escort of at least half a dozen men. I don't know that I can spare that many."

He idly traced the contours of her breasts. The hollows were damp with sweat. A nipple puckered instantly at the touch of his finger.

Sally shivered and turned toward him, putting her

hand on his chest. Just that little gesture made her sigh with pleasure. She inched closer, looking up at him with lambent, smoldering ardor. Fargo wasn't sure that he'd ever put such a glow in a woman's eyes before.

"You know we're just getting to the worst of it," he went on quickly, feeling a little uncomfortable with the rapturous expression on her face. "From now on every step we make will be a step farther into Indian country."

She nodded solemnly as her hand came up to caress his bearded jaw. She wriggled up against him with her soft belly squirming right into his tightly muscled abdomen. Fargo felt his shaft rise up diligently to separate them. It jutted into her belly, large and hard and impossible to deny.

"Dammit, Sally. If you're still hot, we'll get to it, by and by, but we've got some things to discuss."

"My friends," she murmured as her hand inched between them. She sucked up her breath and pressed her fingers in where her belly had been.

"Oh, to hell with it," Fargo cursed. She was right in position. He grabbed her ass, lifted her up, and then rammed her down over his thrumming erection in one smooth motion.

"Oh, God," she gasped as he pushed his entire length into her.

It was as much as some women could take, but Sally didn't seem to have any problem. There was never any need to pet Sally into passion; she was as ready and willing a woman as Fargo had ever encountered. A man merely needed to breathe on her to make her slick inside. But she was tight, too, with a caldron seething beyond her thighs, roiling and tumultuous.

Fargo rolled Sally onto her back and paused, letting her turbulence foment him. She was not only as hot as she had been the first time, she was far more animated. She was excited, restless, and insanely desperate. "Oh, God, oh, God, oh, please," she cried.

Fargo was less driven and more aware this time. He

pushed himself up on his hands with his shaft still buried deep between Sally's spread legs. She was rabid and thrashing, with her face contorted by effort and her cheeks a brilliant scarlet.

She jolted into him, pitching to right and left beneath him. She curled and writhed and twisted, frantically skewering herself with his shaft, while Fargo marveled at her madness. It was contagious, however. Her fervor expanded on the explosive throbbing in his loins without him doing a blessed thing to help.

"Please, I want it. I want it. I need it," she begged, and her muscles added extra inducement, pumping around his organ with their own plea.

Fargo gave it to her, just five quick punches, but with all of his considerable power behind them. And the pressure burst out of him like a runaway locomotive.

Lanced to the core, Sally screamed as if she'd been torn apart. She kept shrieking, over and over, in perfect tempo to the muscular seizures racking her innards, and nearly loud enough to rouse the leaves on the trees.

Robbed of breath, Fargo rested his cheek next to Sally's hair. He coughed a little bit, but it wasn't an agonizing paroxysm.

"Oh, God, Skye, did I hurt you?" Sally asked.

He wanted to laugh, since she had just been screaming as loud as anyone being disemboweled by the Comanche. But he didn't have the energy. "I'm fine," he assured her. He shifted his weight, but he didn't pull out of her, sensing, as he did, that Sally was always a mite more cooperative when she was preoccupied. "That was nice," he told her.

"Oh, Skye, do you really think so?" Her arms closed around him and her fingers crept up to the hair at the nape of his neck.

"I do. You're a pretty woman. And warm. You've got one hell of a lot more to offer than egg-gathering and milking. You shouldn't sell yourself short."

Fargo reached down to caress the soft flesh of her side. She was plump, but not fat. He felt the wanton curve of her, sloping from waist to hip, and he didn't want her to think he was only lying on top of her because he wanted information. But he needed that information.

"Sally, I truly did appreciate the distraction, but you can't keep sidelining me this way. We really do have something to discuss."

"My friends? Oh, Skye, you're right. I know you're right. You've got every right to know everything, and none of us ever had any business agreeing to keep anything from you. My friends had a lot of nerve even asking me to cover for them if I got caught. What they did was wrong. What we all did was wrong, and I am sorry, Skye. But before I tell you about us, I want you to know that it never had anything to do with anything except escaping from Lilabeth. I swear to you it didn't, but I'm so scared that you'll get mad. Please, Skye, promise me you won't get mad again."

Fargo couldn't quite credit Sally's abrupt turnabout, and suspicion reared its ugly head. He pulled away, expecting to fall right out of her, but he slid out instead, his shaft still semitumescent. He supposed it had something to do with the way her interior pulsed like a beating heart, but it irritated him, nonetheless. Sally made a habit of keeping him from more important pursuits. When she wasn't drugging him, she was still dallying with him.

"What right have you got to make me promise not to get mad before I even hear your story?" he demanded. "And why are you being so agreeable all of a sudden anyway? You think you've finally figured out a lie I might buy?"

"Oh, God, Skye, no. It's not like that," she protested, trying to get her arms back around his neck while staring up at him with eyes roiling with emotion. "I love you. I love you so much. I've never felt this way before, never in my whole life. I knew it the minute I saw you standing in the saloon. You were so tall and handsome, Skye, and when you smiled at me, I melted inside. And I still hurt you, drugging you that way. I still can't believe I did that, but I'd never do anything like that again, I swear." She flung herself against him, burying her face against his shoulder.

"Sally, you can't mean that."

"Oh, but I do. I do love you. And when you made me think about my friends, I realized they didn't have any right expecting me to hold out on you, since they know how I feel. And maybe I'm not much of a woman because I've certainly done some wrong things in the past, but maybe that's just because I never felt this way before, but I do now and I figure if a woman's going to be true to anybody, it should be to the man she loves."

"Sally, what are you talking about?" Fargo tried to extricate himself from Sally's embrace, but she clung on tighter than a wood tick.

"Oh, Skye, don't push me away. Please, don't do that. I don't expect anything from you, I swear. I know a man like you would never marry a woman like me, since a man like you could marry most anyone he wanted to. But I love you, anyway, and that's all I want, is just to be able to love you for a little while. I'll do anything you want, anything you say."

"Good! Then, why don't you get dressed?"

"But we have to talk."

"I've been thinking about that. If you tell me about your friends now, I'd be duty-bound to face them as soon as I got back to the train. And I'm feeling a little tired right now. So why don't you just tell me in the morning?"

Sally glanced up at Fargo apprehensively. "You're not mad?"

He pressed her head back down on his shoulder and ran his fingers through her hair. "It'll be all right," he said, because he wasn't mad at her. He just wished he could be anywhere else right then, north of the Missouri, south of the Mason-Dixon Line, west of the Sierra Nevada. Or even New York City.

8

Fargo hadn't expected to be startled awake by any more of his eerie feelings after finding Sally, since her presence explained the odd whisperings and rustlings he had been hearing in the night. It wasn't quite dawn and he didn't know what had wakened him. He listened.

One of the night watch sang a maudlin ballad, low, husky, and off-key, to soothe the quiet oxen. Camp was by the river in a clearing half a mile from where Fargo and Sally had enjoyed the afternoon. The Little Blue gurgled and the brush rustled.

Fargo patted the other side of his bedroll, then rolled over. "Sally, dammit, where in hell are you?"

Although he whispered, his voice sounded louder in his ears than all 350 oxen. He waited but Sally didn't arrive, which meant she hadn't just gone off to answer a call of nature. He grudgingly pulled on his boots.

Canvas wagon covers gleamed in the moonlight, but otherwise the area was shadowy. Fargo circled the enclosure on the outside. The huge wagons loomed like houses, but with considerable room underneath that couldn't be easily seen.

A voice probed from the darkness. "Halt, who goes there?"

"It's me, Fargo." He stepped out of the wagon's shadow and into the night; the guard followed. "Rogers, is that you? It's good to see you up and about."

"Nothing good about it. Hurts too much to try to sleep, so I volunteered for night watch. Mr. Fargo, do your lungs ache like somebody kicked in all your ribs?"

"They smart some," Fargo admitted. "You seen anything besides me?"

"No."

"Well, if you see someone, don't shoot, but make sure you waylay them."

Rogers grinned. "I wouldn't shoot Miss Mason, Mr. Fargo."

Fargo stalked off. Everyone must have heard him calling for her. They doubtlessly thought it was real amusing that Sally had wandered off, since they certainly didn't think it was fair that the wagon master had a woman when they didn't.

It just went to show how much it meant for Sally to claim she'd be true. Her first night in the open, she was missing and Rogers was smirking. As wagon master, Fargo had every right to discipline Rogers for his insolence. "Hell, I should just put him in charge of the woman. That would show him. Then she could make a laughingstock out of him, not me."

Something white was creeping close to the ground beneath the wagon just ahead. Sally had worn a white linen nightgown last night, the kind of ordinary, prim attire no man would expect on a whore. Keeping an eye on the crawling under the next wagon, Fargo dropped back to where he couldn't be seen.

It had to be Sally. His men had no cause for crawling under the wagons, and a thieving Indian would have been more efficient. Besides, nobody but Sally would have worn white, the only color that could show in the void beneath the wagon.

Sally got to the end of the wagon and bumped the chain as she tried to rise. Any of the men would have known exactly where those chains were, since they all helped put them there. Back on hands and knees, she disappeared under the next wagon, where only an occasional blur betrayed her position.

Fargo followed stealthily.

After her clash with the chain, she crawled from wagon to wagon. She moved slowly at first, as dawn began to gild the sky. Before long the men would be up. Sally again tried to hurry.

She would move along at a goodly clip and then

falter clumsily, probably because it wasn't easy to crawl while wearing a long gown. Every few minutes she halted; Fargo figured it was to jerk her nightgown back over her knees. She arrived at her destination, a huge wagon designed to carry four tons of mining machinery. She peered right and left and fore and aft, but didn't see Fargo as he lurked in the shadows.

Bigger than a Conestoga or even a Murphy, the freight wagon wasn't made for easy access. Sally scrambled up the tailgate, but there was no foothold. She was sliding back off it when several arms reached out to help her in.

Fargo sprinted to the wagon, but the voices within were hushed. He drew his Colt and waited. Sally emerged first, landing in an inelegant sprawl. Another woman followed, landing on her feet.

"What in hell?" Fargo exploded. "Hold it right there."

"Oh, God," Sally blurted, straightening despite Fargo's order. "Oh, God, Skye. I didn't, you didn't, I had to, I'm sorry. I'm so sorry," she blurted before bursting into tears.

"You're always sorry, dammit. Do you expect that to help?"

Fargo stared beyond Sally at the woman who had heeded his order to stay put, until then. She stepped forward and put her arms around Sally. The woman was considerably taller than the plump little Sally, but it was hard to see much else about her while she stood in the shadows of the two chained wagons.

"I take it this is your Skye Fargo?" she asked Sally.

Sally sniffled her assent, just as a third body hurtled out of the wagon.

"I don't believe it," Fargo muttered. "If any more are in there, best they come out now, before I blow them full of holes."

"There isn't anyone else," the tall woman volunteered.

Fargo aimed the Colt at the canvas, but no one so much as squealed. The woman was probably telling the truth. He was satisfied, because he wasn't about to turn his back on these three to climb into the wagon.

The last woman out sat on her ass in the dust, with her knees up and her hands flat on the ground to either side of her. She wasn't going for a weapon, so Fargo turned his attention back to the tall woman comforting Sally.

"What's going on here?"

"What does it look like, Mr. Fargo? Isn't it obvious? We've stolen away on your train."

"Which of my men know about this?"

"None," the woman answered.

"You expect me to believe that?"

"You may as well. Do you think Sally would have risked bringing us food and helping us get out to stretch, if one of your men had been available?"

The sky was graying and men were rising. The general level of commotion increased steadily as the animals took to bawling instead of lowing, and the men grumbled and cursed almost as loudly. They were no more eager than the oxen to get the day started.

"Come on," Fargo ordered in sudden decision. A bit of a loner, he always camped a ways from the others, and his men respected his privacy. Where he cast his bedroll was inviolate, a no-trespassing zone except in emergencies. His men wouldn't grant him nearly as much consideration if they saw him standing between the wagons with three women.

"I'm not sure we should go with you," the tall woman objected. "Where are you taking us?"

Fargo balked at her insolence. "To hell—if you don't cooperate. Leastwise, I think that's where you'll end up after I shoot you."

The tall woman considered that for several seconds before falling into position before him. As they walked to his bedroll, Sally renewed her weeping, and the quiet one who had been sitting in the dirt brushed at her skirts and patted at her hair. The tall one spoke.

"Sally, you can quit your crying. I'm doing what the man says. You know, Mr. Fargo, you're exactly the type of man I expected poor Sally to fall for."

"Doesn't sound like a compliment."

"No. Sally's a dear child, but she's not much given to common sense."

"A dear child?" Fargo scoffed. "And you think Sally's got poor judgment." He halted. "Here," he indicated, pointing at his bedroll. "All of you sit." He pulled up a wooden box he had requisitioned for a stool and sat down himself. He towered over the women huddling on his bedroll; he could see them clearly, now that the sky had brightened to mild blue-gray.

They were a mess. The tall woman was blond and blue-eyed and potentially as pretty as a mountain glade. Although she was likely past thirty, she was made to ripen well. She was slender and fine-featured with high breasts, but her plain shirtwaist was filthy, as were her hair and face.

The other woman was dark-haired and voluptuous, shaped like Sally, although the resemblance ended there. Her heavy eye makeup was smeared, making her resemble a raccoon. The black lace trim on her red satin dress had torn away from her plunging neckline to pinpoint her breasts like bull's-eyes on two targets. Huge salt stains circled her armpits.

Sally was dirty from crawling under the wagons, although, as usual, her miserable condition didn't detract from her wide-eyed appeal. She was pathetically cute, even with her tear tracks and splotched cheeks. She huddled against the blond woman's breast while gazing up at Fargo and shivering, her whipped-puppy pose at full intensity.

"Please, Skye," she sniffled, "try to understand. We couldn't stay at Lilabeth's any longer. I told you about Lilabeth. Why, she and Harry didn't even run a proper house, just a saloon with private rooms, but she charged us like she did, demanded extra if a girl spent ten minutes overtime with a gent. She even wanted two hundred dollars for the five days I spent with you, and that wasn't fair at all, since you weren't one of her customers, you were my friend."

"All right," Fargo snapped. "So Lilabeth's a bitch. That doesn't explain why you're here. This is a freight train, not a rolling whorehouse."

"But, Skye, the stage isn't running west right now, and surely you can see that women like us can't go east. Towns farther east make it hard for women like us to make an honest living, but we had to get out right away. Just last week Lilabeth and Harry had poor Myra, here, arrested." Sally nodded at the blonde. "Lilabeth charged her with running off with goods belonging to the Paradise at Trail's End Saloon, which I suppose was true, since Myra was wearing her costume when she ran off, but it wasn't fair."

"Look, Mr. Fargo," the blond woman broke in imperiously. "We do have a little money, and we're quite prepared to pay for our passage."

"But this isn't a stagecoach, honey. It's a freight train. We don't haul passengers."

"But you have passengers, Mr. Fargo. And as for the stagecoach, if it were running, I assure you we would have taken it. Your accommodations are deplorable."

"My accommodations?" Fargo spluttered, standing up and glowering down on her. "I'm not offering accommodations, and you damn well better not be expecting any."

"Oh, no, we're not," Sally piped in. "Please, Skye, don't send us back to Leavenworth. Lilabeth claims we owe her a fortune. She'd have us arrested for sure. And you know about the authorities, always on the side of big business. And Lilabeth already bribes the man who checks on the saloons—so he'd testify against us. Oh, God, it isn't fair," she lamented tearfully. "Why, the way it works, I'm the one who really has to pay that man, and he's such a creepy little pervert."

Myra hugged Sally more tightly. "Shut up," she ordered. "And quit whining. Don't you ever learn anything? You were always whining at Lilabeth's, too, and a fat lot of good it did you. You always got the worst men. But, then, maybe you liked it that way," the blonde lectured sternly. "After all, you picked this one, and although he may be a handsome buck, he doesn't strike me as any more reasonable than Lilabeth."

Myra turned to the Trailsman, and her blue eyes glittered with challenge. "Or am I mistaken, Mr. Fargo? Will you escort us to Denver or won't you? We shall, of course, recompense you for our passage and any undue inconvenience it entails—if you have the decency to do what is obviously the right thing, considering how you cheated poor Sally back in Leavenworth."

"I cheated Sally?" Fargo blurted. "Do you know what she did?"

"Of course I know what she did," Myra bristled. "Perhaps it was unfortunate, but Sally was quite desperate. Lilabeth claims we owe her eight hundred dollars. And Harry, the bastard, goes along with whatever Lilabeth says. Mr. Fargo, do you know what it's like to work day and night and always fall farther behind? Of course not," she denied. "Why, you couldn't even imagine the work we do—since men have no stamina whatsoever."

"Goddamn. Now I remember. You're the Myra with the herbs. You were in on having me drugged. Talk about the pot calling the kettle black. Just where do you get off rawhiding me? You'd better be careful, honey. Because if you don't take it easy, I'll take that money of yours and then I'll sell you to the Indians for buffalo robes. I'd make a tidy little profit."

Cowering behind the other two, the quiet woman made her presence known by gasping as Sally pitched into a new fit of sobbing.

"You have no cause to threaten us," Myra responded coldly.

"Really?" Fargo asked. The truth was that he admired Myra's courage more than the other women's cowering, but Myra was not a passenger on this train. She was an unwelcome burden, entirely under the command of Skye Fargo and not even entitled to make requests, let alone demands. The sooner she understood that, the better. "Henceforth, you'll follow my orders without question or be turned out. Do you understand?"

"I shall cause no trouble if we're graciously treated."

"Graciously treated?" Fargo repeated, not believing that the woman had the nerve to keep baiting him. "You'll be treated like what you are. Illegal freight."

"In that case, perhaps I should leave now."

"Go ahead. But I hope you know what the Indians will do if they find you. They share their captives. Twenty, thirty, fifty of them, however many warriors show up for the fun."

Myra raised her brow. "You think I couldn't handle that?"

"They're not gentle, honey."

"Neither are Lilabeth's patrons, Mr. Fargo. So, if you are trying to frighten us, don't bother. As you can see, Sally and Daisy are already frightened, and I am not about to get that way."

Three women on his train could cause a degree of distraction his men couldn't afford, unless those women were absolutely controlled. Fargo pointed at Myra. "Come with me. We need a private talk about how 'gracious' treatment goes two ways."

Myra was slim and willowy and looked almost fragile, but she asserted a determination the others didn't possess. Still, Fargo thought he saw a crack in her resolve as she licked her lips before she announced, "Any discussion of our treatment concerns all of us. I prefer that we discuss it together."

"Is that so?" Leaning down, Fargo grabbed Myra's arm and jerked her to her feet.

"Yes, it's so," she said, digging in her heels. She jutted out her jaw with a stubbornness a mule would have envied.

Fargo hoisted her up like a feed sack and threw her over his shoulder.

"For God's sake, help me," Myra commanded the other women.

Fargo swung around to address Sally and Daisy. "You two have a choice: you can listen to Myra, or you can listen to me."

"Yes, sir," Daisy said, putting her hand to her bosom and fingering herself in a frankly suggestive manner while she fixed Fargo with a flirting look.

Meanwhile, Myra kicked viciously and pounded on Fargo's back.

Sally bounded to her feet. "Oh, Skye, oh, Myra, oh, please," Sally babbled as she rushed to intervene. "Please, Skye, please don't hurt her."

"Me, hurt her?" Fargo bellowed as Sally was forced to step back to avoid Myra's swinging feet. "Sally, sit back down."

Sally gazed at him glumly with her ever-ready tears pooling in her eyes. "Oh, Myra, I'm sorry," she said before resuming her seat.

As Myra twisted and turned, Fargo whirled and strode off with her.

"Put me down this instant," she yelled.

"Sure enough, sweetheart. As soon as you figure out who's boss around here, I'll put you down."

She was scared, more scared than a woman like her would ever let on. He could feel the tremors in her body, the trembling in her hands as they pushed at his back. Myra bucked up high and Fargo clamped his palm firmly on her ass.

"Whoa," he cautioned. "You don't want to get thrown, do you, honey? So just calm down." He caressed Myra's ass because it was the portion of her anatomy directly underhand. But it was a mistake.

She stiffened momentarily, then renewed her efforts at escape by trying to scramble down Fargo's back, without a thought that if she was successful she would break her neck.

"Cut it out," Fargo bellowed, reaching up under her skirt to grasp a thigh, since he didn't trust the material of her dress not to give way if she plunged headfirst toward the ground.

She was scared, all right. The muscles of her thigh spasmed beneath his grip and she shivered all over. But she responded like a cornered dog, all snarls and claws.

"Why, you poorly petered, half-hung, limp-peckered gelding, let me go."

"Limp-peckered?" Fargo retorted. "And just how would you know, honey? Or are you asking to find out?"

"I don't need to find out. I know Sally. Though I love her dearly, she doesn't have an iota of sense, a modicum of taste, or a spoonful of brains."

"I'll have to remember to tell her you said so," Fargo commented dryly.

"Why, you pussy-licking, impotent scum-scrotum," Myra roared, launching a stream of oaths.

"Listen, sweetheart," Fargo soothed loudly so he could be heard above Myra's heated imprecations. "I'm not going to hurt you. I'm just going to take you to where we can talk privately. I think maybe we got off on the wrong foot."

"We didn't get off on the wrong foot," Myra screeched as she renewed her assault on Fargo's back. "You got off on the wrong woman. Sally may be a fool, but if you think I'm just going to let you have your lay without the pay, you're wrong. I'll make you pay, Mr. Fargo. Rape me if you want. Kill me if you must. Leave me out here for all I care. But I'm not going to make it pleasant for you. I'm through with being an easy mark for men like you and Harry. Do you hear me, Mr. Fargo? I'm through. Maybe you can make me do what you want, but it won't be fun."

Fargo jerked the woman up higher, so that her hips, rather than her waist, were draped across his shoulder.

Screaming invectives, Myra tried to grab at his ass as she swung. "Why, you whoremongering, peanut-cocked son of a bitch," she wailed as her forehead banged against his belt. "When I get down, I'll tear your worthless balls right out of their sockets."

"What's wrong with you, anyway?" Fargo shouted. "In case you haven't noticed, you're in no position to threaten me."

But Myra was lost to reason. She was wild with fear and fury. Fargo wondered if she was ever that energetic in bed, but pushed the thought aside as she tried to bite him. Her teeth connected only with his shirt, so she spit instead. Fargo grimaced as the warm wetness soaked through the flannel just above his waist.

He had planned on getting Myra away from the others in order to reason with her about the way things would have to be for all their sakes. He had planned to take her to a grassy spot along the river where a few small cottonwoods would shield their argument from the others, a calm place where maybe he could get her to admit that mutiny wasn't the best stratagem for stowaways. But there was no reasoning with the woman.

He halted on the bank of the Little Blue. Grasping Myra's hips, he pulled her down before him, scooped up her knees, and dropped her into the water. Although the river wasn't more than knee-deep, all of her went under.

"Why, you . . ." she spluttered as she surfaced.

Fargo grinned as the obscenities gushed out. "I just thought one of us should cool off, honey. Since you seemed to be the hottest . . ." He shrugged, turned around, and started back toward the wagons. He had a train to run.

Despite their grumbling earlier, this was mostly a day of rest for both men and oxen. Only the repair crew assigned to Old Will was going to be busy—trying to get the two stamp-carrying wagons back together.

Fargo found Amos inspecting a wheel hub. "You hear from Old Will's crew?" he asked.

Amos straightened and nodded. "They think they'll have 'em ready to run by this afternoon."

"Then we can leave in the morning?"

"Yep."

"Amos, I've got a problem I've got to discuss with you. Two problems, actually. I think we'd better put our heads together." Fargo gestured toward his own campsite and the two men started walking that way.

"This got something to do with Sally?" Amos asked.

"Maybe we'd better make that three problems," Fargo said. "It seems that Sally brought some friends along, a woman named Daisy and a woman named Myra."

"Myra?" Amos halted in midstride. He looked thunderstruck.

"I take it you've met her." Fargo laughed. "What a kicking, screaming shrew. Granted, I scared her some, but the bitch has the temperament of a rabid dog."

"Myra?"

"Myra. A blond woman about thirty, tall and thin, real pretty, but not worth the trouble, a bitch with a bullwhacker's tongue. You know her, right?"

"Well, sure. But she ain't like that." As always, Amos had trouble keeping his mind on the conversation. He turned and scanned the wagon enclosure. His eyes narrowed, his attention riveted on the train. "Wait a minute, Skye. I'll be right back." Amos bounded off, a huge man who could cover territory with surprising speed.

Today was already turning into another scorcher. The morning sun hadn't really taken hold of the sky yet, but their clearing was heating up like a forge. Fargo simmered until Amos returned.

"That canvas was loose," Amos explained. He pointed back at a wagon. "So I set somebody to fixing it."

"Amos, we've got more important problems."

"Well, sure, but . . ." Amos shrugged and turned his attention to the scenery. He studied it as if he might find an Indian lurking in the grass—which wasn't entirely impossible, but there were guards. Besides, the Trailsman had already eyeballed that possibility.

Fargo was beginning to understand Winfield. "All right. Come clean, Amos. What is it you don't want to tell? Did you know the women were on the train?"

"No."

"You suspected?"

"No. Well, I mean . . . Well, at night there were funny noises sometimes. I was always getting up to investigate. But I thought maybe the men were getting into a little whiskey or something. Didn't suspect nothing more serious."

"But?" Fargo prodded.

"Oh, hell, Skye. I think maybe the women being here is my fault. Thought it was yours. Thought Sally had tagged after you. But Myra too?"

"You and Myra have something special?"

"No. At least, not the way you mean. I gave her money, that's all. Would have given some to Sally too if I'd thought she could hang on to it."

"You gave her money? Why?"

"Because Lilabeth's a bitch."

"So is Myra."

"No, she ain't."

"Amos, are you sure you know Myra? She's a real virago, screaming, spitting, biting, cursing."

"That ain't like Myra." Amos stopped walking and turned to study Fargo. "Maybe it's because you look a little like Harry."

"Who's Harry?"

"He'd look kind of ordinary next to you, but he's got the same bright-blue eyes. And he's a real lady-killer. Claims he's Lilabeth's brother. But I figure he's really her man. He married Myra in San Francisco."

"Myra's married?"

"Doubt it was legal, since Harry brought the preacher and Myra says he introduced the fellow as a friend."

"Well, I guess none of that is real important," Fargo commented. "The important thing is what we're going to do with the women now. When it was just Sally, I thought we'd bring her along. But three are just too many. It'll take six men to escort them back to Leavenworth. Think we can spare that many?"

"We could if we had to. But you can't do that, Skye."

"Why? Do you think we're going to run into Indian trouble soon?"

"Not that. It's Myra and Sally. You can't send 'em back. Harry might find 'em."

"Harry's not my problem. He's Myra's problem. Hell, she married him."

"Sure. And the only time Harry's ever admitted that is when Lilabeth had Myra arrested. Harry went and bailed her out. Her being his so-called wife made it easy. Then together, Harry and Lilabeth had Myra back at work within an hour. He uses her, beats her, sells her. Skye, I know you. You wouldn't send a woman back to that."

"It's that bad?"

"I guess Myra was just an unhappy, down-on-her-luck whore in San Francisco. Harry claimed to be a wealthy respectable Leavenworth merchant deep in love. But Myra was thrilled, so she got herself into more of a fix than she could handle."

"And you gave her money to get out of it."

"Yeah, but I didn't know she'd come here."

They had gotten to Fargo's campsite, where all three women sat on his bedroll. They were all cleaned up and changed. Under other circumstances, Fargo wouldn't have minded such a comely group occupying his bedroll.

Myra shrieked, jumped up, and ran to Winfield. "Oh, Amos, you're here," she cried, throwing her arms around the big man's broad torso.

Sally stood too, but stayed in place. Daisy watched languidly, apparently neither happy nor unhappy about Winfield's arrival.

"Sally?" Winfield murmured, glancing her way.

"Oh, Amos," she whimpered, glancing nervously at Fargo. "Skye will get the wrong idea."

With Myra still clinging like a baby possum on one side, Amos stepped forward and hugged Sally in his other arm. "You and Myra are here because of me, aren't you?"

Sally stared up at the huge man. "We couldn't think of anywhere else to go."

"What was all this stuff about drugging Skye?"

"You were leaving, Amos. And Myra and me were desperate. But we didn't want you to know things were getting worse, because we were afraid you'd kill Harry. And you hadn't given any money to Myra yet, and so we were broke. Then Webster offered me money, and I told Myra. But we couldn't tell you, because we knew how mad you'd get. But when we thought about it, we couldn't see how taking the money could hurt, because you and Skye Fargo could certainly catch up to any train. But we really made a mess of it, didn't we, Amos? Oh, Amos, are you in as much trouble as we're in?"

Amos looked over Sally's head at Fargo, and then the big man did something the Trailsman had never seen him do before. Winfield laughed. He laughed until both women in his arms were gawking up at him. He laughed until even Daisy gaped at him, and up until now, nothing had inspired much response from Daisy.

"Girls," Amos said to the women in his arms, "Skye and I have a little more to discuss. So you go on over there."

Amos pointed up a path that led to the river. The huge clearing the wagons were in was often used for noonings and Sabbath stopovers, so numerous trails ran every which way through the brush. There were smaller clearings and campsites most everywhere.

"See that fire ring?" Amos asked. "You three go on over there and build a fire. I'll bring some food and utensils in a bit. Is that all right, Skye?" Amos blurted abruptly. Winfield was obviously accustomed to being in charge.

"It's fine," Fargo assented.

Amos turned a stern eye on Daisy. "This is a freight train, so you won't be eating with the men. And I don't want you mingling with them under any circumstances, understand?"

Sally and Myra were effusive with their assurances, but Daisy just smiled. Fargo watched the women walk off. Sally, short, plump and bouncy. Myra, tall, with a gentle sway. Daisy, slow and indolent.

"Amos, I'm going to have to leave you with them. Somebody lit that prairie fire. I've got to go find out who."

"I figured you'd have to go sooner or later. When?"

"Is tomorrow too soon?"

"Well, yes." Staring off in the direction the women

had taken, Amos sat on the supply box Fargo had used as a stool earlier. "But I reckon I can handle it, although it's sure going to be more to handle than I figured on when I signed up."

"You're sure?" Fargo asked anxiously. "You've still got the burn-out to get through. But I've got this feeling I shouldn't wait on this. The women? Hell, I don't see any good way to handle them."

"I don't think Sally and Myra will be a problem," Amos commented. "But Daisy? I suspect they only brought her because she threatened to rat to Harry. Bet money she plans on lining her pockets by screwing a whole train's worth of men. She's always been Harry and Lilabeth's shill, and she plays things their way. Keeping Daisy out of trouble won't be easy."

A thunderous explosion rent the air. Amos jumped to his feet, Fargo whirled, and Sally and Myra came screeching back into camp as smoke billowed from a wagon.

"What is it?" Myra demanded.

"Oh, God," Sally whimpered.

Amos was already sprinting toward the wagon enclosure, but Fargo hesitated. Several yards away, Daisy sat placidly by the women's campfire. Fargo noted her there before he dashed off.

9

They were lucky again. The entire right side of one wagon had been blown away. Several blackened beams lay on the ground amid a fan of debris. But only one man had been injured, and he could be fixed with tweezers and bandages.

Fargo crouched beside one burned beam. The ground around him was strewn with tatters of canvas and bits of white oak, splintered into toothpicks. He put his fingers to the charred beam and scratched, studied, tasted.

"Amos, divide the men into groups of three and have them check all the wagons. Look for black powder. Smell for it."

"That's what it was?" Amos asked.

"Somebody poured it into the cracks between the boards." He turned and eyed the wrecked wagon. All four wheels were intact, so it still sat high, with just a gaping hole to show for its trouble. It wouldn't be easy to repair out here, without extra lumber, but it could be done.

On the inside were supports of some sort. Though Fargo wasn't sure what they were for, they were big chunks of metal arched like bridges, and they had come all the way from an eastern foundry and were thus irreplaceable. Cast iron could be brittle enough to shatter. But it hadn't—this time. When Fargo investigated, the metal had felt smooth, without fractures, pitting, or heat damage.

The explosion had blown outward, ripping the right side from the wagon, but leaving little real damage.

The cargo, wheels, base, brakes, tongue, and axles were virtually untouched. They had been lucky again, but the Trailsman didn't like to rely on luck.

It was the same wagon the women had been in, but he couldn't make a connection. Even if they had poured powder into the cracks, they hadn't been around to light it. An accomplice, perhaps?

He turned his attention back to the debris. Some glittered like fool's gold. He sifted some of the glinting fragments through his fingers. Patient and determined, he crawled around on his hands and knees until he found a sliver of silvered glass.

It was embedded in his palm. "Shit," Fargo muttered, pulling it out. He stared at it, a shard almost a half-inch long. "But that's crazy," he told himself.

Sally was running toward him, screeching and flapping her arms. "Skye, she's gone," Sally shouted.

"Who's gone?"

"Daisy. She said she was going to the river, but she's not there, and Myra said to get you. Oh, Skye, do you think it was Indians? Do you think they'll get Myra, too?"

"No. Where's Myra?"

"She said she was going after them. But I don't see how, since they were already gone. I asked, but she just told me not to be a ninny. And then she took off, shouting back that I should get you, not Amos, but you."

Fargo sprinted toward the river and Sally did her best to keep up.

"Is Myra armed?" he asked.

"She has a derringer, and a knife. Always carries them," Sally huffed.

"That's nice to know. Wish I'd known sooner."

"I don't know if it's nice. It didn't help with Harry. 'Course, Myra couldn't kill him; she would have been arrested. Skye," Sally cried, "I can't keep up."

"Good, go back to Amos."

"But Skye—"

"Now," he ordered, leaving Sally behind as he poured on speed.

Fargo thrashed through the brush beside the river and splashed into the water. He scanned the bank. He spotted Myra first, running along the riverside path, her tall form appearing and then disappearing in a stand of bur oak. He scouted ahead. The cottonwoods were thicker up there. He squinted.

"Goddamn. Horses," Fargo grunted, already streaking back toward camp.

He didn't take time to saddle his Ovaro, but mounted Indian-style in a flying leap. He overtook Myra within minutes. "Go back to camp," he ordered, flashing past.

"No," she shouted.

"Goddamn bitch," he cursed as he urged the pinto on. He caught sight of a horse's rump, just a quick glimpse far down the trail, before it disappeared behind a clump of chokecherry. It was too far for the Colt, and Fargo's Sharps was back at camp. His adversaries had arrived better equipped, however.

A shot thundered, whizzing so close Fargo could feel its vibration sending chills down his spine. Since he was barely in range, he pulled back, grasping the Ovaro with his knees and his arms. A shot followed and Fargo whirled the animal around, manhandling the pinto in the absence of reins and bridle.

"No sense riding into an ambush," Fargo told his horse. "Besides, that guy is good."

Another shot reverberated. It was from a different gun, a repeater, Fargo surmised instantly, a seven-shot Spencer from the sound of it. More loud reports and bullets followed in quick succession to prove his split-second surmise. He prodded the pinto away.

It was much harder to get the Ovaro halted the second time, since the horse had a passion for running forward when there were bullets flying behind. Fargo grabbed with his knees, but the pinto was bridle-trained and apparently figured he could ignore his reinless master.

Myra stood smack in the middle of the trail. "Get the hell out of the way," Fargo shouted as he doubled his efforts to control his rampaging mount.

When she finally realized Fargo wasn't going to stop for her, Myra dived into the brush. Meanwhile, the pinto leapt and bounded against the Trailsman's restraining hold. The huge beast pranced and danced skittishly to a halt, sending up plumes of dust, just as Myra ran up looking tousled from her vault into the chokecherries.

"What are you doing running away from them?" she demanded.

Fargo regarded her from atop the shuddering, wild-eyed Ovaro. "You really do have a lot of confidence in me, don't you, honey?"

He turned to the chokecherries and wildflowers, the brush and grass, the bur oaks and the cottonwoods. The river gave the tallgrass prairie a touch of woodland spirit.

A half-mile away, the main trail paralleled the river trail. Narrow footpaths ran back and forth, here and there, between them. With so many routes, it was more like a city park than a wilderness, but few of the little byways, with their low-hanging limbs and their meandering ways, were suitable for a horse.

But Fargo's best bet was to beat the other horsemen back to the main trail and meet them there. Going all the way back to the wagon enclosure to take the best road to the main trail would mean going a mile out of his way, and then he would have to cover that extra mile again. The horse shivered a bit, but seemed to remember who was boss now that there weren't bullets aimed at his tail.

Fargo glared down at Myra. "Go back now. Do you understand? You keep going on and I'll tie you to a tree."

She glared back at him, but then she turned and started walking just as Fargo kicked the Ovaro back toward the gunmen.

He veered off the path and headed directly into a

stand of blue vervain. More cautious than his master, the relieved pinto picked up speed. As they left the dreaded route toward the gunmen, the horse's hooves bit into the wildflowers, sending violet blossoms flying in every direction.

Leaning low, Fargo urged the horse cross-country. If he could get to the main trail—and figure out where the others had to come out on it—he could lie in wait, and thus the disadvantage of not having a rifle would be somewhat nullified.

The land dipped and the pinto flew. "Oh, shit," Fargo swore. Suddenly visible was a small creek banked by low shrubs. A wild tangled thicket rose before them, no more than five feet high, but with glossy leaves and stems reaching out to snag the pinto's hooves. The bushes edged both sides of a tiny stream, forming a solid barrier. How wide they spread, Fargo couldn't rightly tell, since he was hurtling straight toward them.

Maybe they were too wide, maybe they were only a yard across, maybe they were several. The Ovaro surged ahead, apparently less daunted by walls than bullets. But the pinto was no steeplechaser. Fargo's decision was instant, because there wasn't enough time or room left to change it.

With no saddle, no reins, and no stirrups, he clung like a Comanche, hoping he had learned something from observing those horsemen of the plains, but not at all sure it would be enough.

Fargo visualized the jump in his mind, he shifted subtly to bring the horse level, shifted again to bring the front quarters down as the hindquarters soared. He was part of the horse, an extension of the pinto's power and speed as they sailed right over the creek and kept on racing.

The path narrowed and the grass got thicker and higher. They arrived at the main road and turned west. About a mile away, he found the trail he was looking for, a broader, better-cleared way down to the river. He dismounted and checked the dirt. It was the way Daisy's friends had come in the first place.

Fargo was sure they were Daisy's friends, and he was sure she had been expecting them. In all probability, they had been lurking nearby for days, awaiting her escape. Like as not, they had set the prairie fire.

Because he could see no reason to put his horse in the line of fire, Fargo jogged across the main trail. He led his Ovaro into the tallgrass, prompting the animal back into the thick growth until the horse was concealed. Then he bounded back across the road and took up his own place, hidden in the grass, flat on his belly alongside the smaller trail.

They came, four horsemen, two sets of two men riding abreast, with Daisy riding double with the man on the left rear horse. They were walking their mounts and talking, in no particular hurry after driving Fargo back.

The Trailsman waited for them to pass. "All right," he shouted. "Drop your weapons and put up your hands. I've got you covered."

They responded predictably, going for their guns, although they didn't have a chance, Fargo was at their back and had the drop on them. He took the left lead out before the man's hand reached his pistol.

Seeing the man in front of her go down, Daisy panicked and tried to use her riding partner for refuge. She twisted and lunged behind the man, trying to push him out in front of her, but the man shoved her off. She fell between the horses, screaming.

By then it was a real melee. The left lead horse was confused by a downed rider with his foot caught in the stirrup. The beast curled up its back and bounced like a bronco, while the right lead rider tried to reel his horse around to face Fargo. The man behind raged abuse at both of them, while Daisy's partner was getting the hell out of there by galloping right into the tallgrass.

"Stop," Fargo ordered.

Still moving, albeit slowly due to stringy grass that was tougher than it looked, the man got off a wild shot. Fargo's was true. The rider lurched forward just as the horse bounded sideways to get back on the road. The man slid off clean and the horse went tearing away.

The other two men were still entwined in a snarl of frightened horseflesh. They were shouting and Daisy was screaming. Fargo couldn't figure out why she hadn't been trampled into jelly. The woman was on her feet, pulling at one rider's legs as she attempted to mount his horse. He was kicking at her and seeking to maim the Trailsman at the same time. But they had all been churning around too much to know where Fargo lay in the grass. The man's shots flew high and far to the right.

The Trailsman calculated his own aim more carefully. The bullet slammed into the middle of the man's chest, making a very small hole that didn't look to amount to anything, but the man fell within the second, landing atop Daisy.

Having disposed of its burden, the bucking horse took off like greased lightning, leaving the last rider clear to escape.

"Halt," Fargo commanded.

"No," the rider protested, forgetting his gun entirely as he leaned low and spurred his horse.

Since it didn't seem sporting to shoot the man in the back, even if he was a cowardly bastard, Fargo let him go. "Tell your boss man that next time none of you go free," he hollered after him.

Before Fargo could leave the brush, hooves were pounding up the main trail. He tensed, readying himself for another armed encounter. The horse skittered to a stop and the rider bounded off.

"Dear God," Myra said, taking in the three bodies lying in the road.

"What in hell are you doing here?"

"You're all right," she said, looking more than a little dazed. "I brought you this," she added, holding out his Sharps.

"That's nice. But I've done enough hunting for today." Fargo walked past her, over to the dead man who had landed on Daisy. He had either crushed the woman or she had fainted. Fargo grabbed the corpse under the armpits.

"Why, Daisy is under him," Myra said, staring down at the woman's legs sticking out from under the huge man's body. The rest of Daisy was covered.

"Help me with him, he's heavy."

If Fargo had expected Myra to balk, he was disappointed. Instead, she tried to tug the man's ankles, but he was too big and she was too light. She couldn't lift his deadweight knee-high.

"Oh, hell, forget it," Fargo advised as he tried to roll the corpse off Daisy.

But Myra was no quitter. She moved to the man's knees and scooped them up like a bundle of wood. Together, they managed to roll the man aside—and plenty of man he was too, potbellied, beefy, joweled.

Daisy hadn't fainted, after all. She was merely holding her breath.

"You hurt?" Fargo asked.

"I don't think so," she whispered as she sat up and took slow breaths as if she feared her ribs may have suffered displacement.

"Well, you don't look so good, but I don't think you're hurt, either," Fargo agreed. "You've got blood on your face and dirt in your hair, but that can be fixed. Too bad you don't have a mirror, though. But then you broke yours, didn't you?"

Daisy glanced up at him fearfully.

"Why?" he demanded.

"It was an accident."

"Dammit, I know it wasn't an accident. You stuffed powder thick in the cracks, especially the big gap between the sideboard and the base, and then you tossed pieces of mirror around where you knew—from spending days in that wagon—that it would catch the sun and reflect it down onto the planks. But it was a miracle that it worked. It could have just as easily been discovered without ever causing a problem."

"But I knew I was getting away today, so it was worth a chance."

"That's where you miscalculated. You aren't going anywhere, Daisy."

"Mr. Fargo, I supposed Daisy had something to do with that explosion as soon as I realized that she was gone," Myra interjected. "But how could she have done it? When could she have done it?"

"In the two or three minutes it took her to jump out of that wagon after you and Sally. She had it planned. But she must have used an accelerant of some sort. Something that burned up so well I couldn't figure it. You going to help me, Daisy? What was it?"

"Why should I help you?" she asked sullenly.

"Beats me," he admitted. "Because it won't get you anywhere. Truth is, you're in big trouble."

"It was coal oil," Myra said.

"How would you know?"

"Because she had this big bottle of perfume." Myra held her hands up to indicate a quart-sized bottle. "I told her she had better not use it with all of us crushed in there like packaged crackers. But later, when we all began to smell rather pungent, I thought perhaps perfume wasn't such a bad idea, after all. Daisy was asleep, but I didn't think it would matter if I borrowed a little—except it wasn't perfume. It was coal oil."

The fat corpse looked bloated with death, although he hadn't been gone long enough for the gases to build within. Even though Daisy didn't look nonplussed or even upset about sitting so close to a cadaver, Fargo turned away from the disgusting sight and went over to inspect the next body.

The man lay on his side, curled into a fetal position, as if to avoid the hooves. His defensive position hadn't worked. The man's hip was crushed into a pulp of bone, blood, and cloth. Another hoof had driven right through to the man's intestines. It was the rider who had been dragged slightly and bounced considerably, and his shoulder was awkwardly scrunched up because of it.

Fargo rolled the body with the toe of his boot. The man was small, skinny, red-haired, and very dead, although the horse had had as much to do with that as Fargo had. The bullet that had sent the man down had plowed into his back and maybe even snared a lung. The hit was debilitating, perhaps even lethal, but it wouldn't have killed immediately.

"Goddamn, it's Chatham," Fargo said.

Myra was beside him in an instant. "Why, it is."

"What does Chatham have to do with this?"

"I don't know," Myra answered.

"But you know, don't you, Daisy?" Fargo accused, spinning to scowl down on her.

The woman sat in the dirt, filthy, mussed up, and streaked with blood, but wearing the arrogant condescending smirk that eastern lawyers generally put on. "I've got no reason to tell you anything," she said.

Fargo drew the Colt. "You want to join your friends?"

Daisy's eyes flickered to the fat corpse, to Chatham, and then to her other unfortunate acquaintances. She paled and trembled, but her chin came up. "You wouldn't do that to a woman."

"You're betting on it?" Fargo asked casually.

Not able to meet the Trailsman's challenge in the eye, Daisy dropped her head.

The afternoon was growing hot and flies buzzed around the corpses while Daisy wavered. For a moment, the world was all static and deceptively calm while Daisy and Fargo pitted themselves in a battle of wills. Then Daisy's round little face tilted up with foolish hauteur fairly glowing from it. "Yes, I'm betting on it. You won't shoot me, Mr. Fargo."

He was angry enough to chew iron and spit nails. He was sorely tempted, but she was right. He couldn't shoot an unarmed woman.

"Well, do something, Fargo," Myra commanded.

"What do you want me to do?" he chafed. "Give her a black eye?"

"That wouldn't be such a bad idea," Myra answered.

Suddenly Myra whipped up her skirt and took a wicked blade out of a sheath strapped onto her slender thigh, next to her garter.

"What are you doing?" Fargo wondered.

"What does it look like?" Myra countered, whirling back toward Daisy. Myra strode to the woman.

Daisy cringed. She began to rise, but she was more bruised than she figured. She moved slowly, too slowly. Myra snatched Daisy's hair and dropped behind her, bringing the knife up against the dark-haired woman's neck.

"Now, tell us about Chatham," Myra urged.

"I won't."

Fargo wouldn't have ignored that grim set to Myra's face, but Daisy couldn't see it.

"Well, good," Myra seethed, levering her blade into Daisy's flesh. Blood trickled down her pudgy neck.

"Stop her," Daisy screeched. "You can't let her do this, Mr. Fargo."

Fargo almost did stop Myra, since it was disconcerting to see a woman so bloodthirsty. Then he remembered that he had asked Daisy a question himself. "Well, maybe I will, as soon as you tell us about Chatham."

"I won't," she screamed.

"You will," Myra said tightly, nudging the knife.

Blood slowly pooled along the blade, then dripped and trickled across Daisy's shoulder. It followed the curve of her breast, a scarlet rivulet running to her cleavage. The blood seeped down between the woman's breasts to form a growing stain in the center of Daisy's low-cut champagne silk gown. It wasn't much blood. Fargo had seen boys slash themselves deeper to become blood brothers. But it had its effect on Daisy.

"I'd be careful with that knife," Fargo commented dryly. "If Daisy faints into it, she won't be answering questions."

His ploy had the desired effect. Daisy came out of her jaw-gripping, fist-clenching stupor. Her hand flew up to press the stain on her bosom. "My God, you can't do this," she shrieked. "You're animals. That's what you are. Animals."

"Us, animals? Why, you bitch," Myra hissed. "You and Chatham took advantage of Sally and me. Sure you threatened to tell Harry we were leaving, but you also claimed to hate Lilabeth. You cried. You said you had to get away."

"I do hate Lilabeth," Daisy crowed with the lilt of madness. "But she's gone by now."

"Gone?"

"Dead. Harry and me are in this together. We're going to get us one hell of a stake. And you little twits played right into our hands," Daisy hooted triumphantly. She started to turn, but the knife bit, starting a new trickle. Daisy gasped. "Why don't you give it up, Myra?" she choked out. "Skye Fargo's a gentleman. He won't let you really hurt me. Will you, Mr. Fargo?"

Daisy's gaze settled on Fargo, taunting him with her jeering contempt. She used the word "gentleman" as an insult. She seemed to think she could get away with anything, and though she was maddeningly reckless, she wasn't entirely wrong. There were some things a man didn't stoop to, no matter what. Fortunately, Myra was already stooping to those things.

Turning away from Daisy's brazen confrontation, Fargo went over and stared down at the third body, nobody he recognized. "I suppose it depends," Fargo announced judiciously. "I guess it might soothe my conscience to rescue you—if you tell us about Chatham."

"You'll rescue me either way," Daisy boasted. "But I'll tell you about Chatham, since it's no secret anymore. Chatham and me were supposed to create a diversion in camp during the fire, so that Webster's men could ride in. But when Amos found Sally, he started asking around for Chatham. I guess Amos must have seen Chatham do something suspicious earlier, because Lord knows Sally wouldn't have ratted on him, stupid little sap that she is."

"But she did tell on him," Fargo objected.

"Oh, sure, later, after he'd run off. Why, Sally's such an idiot, she never even realized Chatham had put the idea in her head to stow away on your train. All he had to do was whisper a few words about how he was leaving, how he was worried about her, how he wished he could take her with him. And before long, Sally was begging and Chatham was objecting. Of course, Harry thought of all of it. Even told Chatham when to fuck her and when to just hold her hand."

"That bastard," Myra hissed. Her knife hand tensed.

"What kind of diversion were you and Chatham planning?" Fargo asked hastily, not at all sure that Myra wouldn't inflict a sudden and deadly end on his source of information.

"I was going to set fire to as many canvases as I could. That's what the coal oil was for. Chatham was supposed to run off the stock."

"What were Webster and McCormick going to get out of this?"

"Whatever they could." Daisy laughed, but quieted when Myra yanked on her hair and slid the knife slightly forward so that the tip came close to her jugular vein.

"I didn't think that was funny," Myra said.

"It wasn't supposed to be," Daisy growled. "There's lots of money to be made in Indian wars—what with the soldiers running around trying to escort wagons, while half of the settlers have fled east. And if a train like Mr. Fargo's just disappears, you'd better believe they'll blame it on Indians."

"So they're after my train," Fargo mused.

"No," Daisy denied. "That was just a passing fancy. A train's got too many able-bodied men to bother with when there's lots of things out there that aren't guarded at all, sitting out there for the taking."

"If they're not after my train, then why are they hounding me? Webster and McCormick were out to get me before I ever left Leavenworth."

"Oh, don't play the babe with me Mr. High and Mighty Do-gooder Fargo—sneaking and spying all over our camp, asking a thousand questions and talking to all the men. Combine trains? Do you really think Harry's such a sucker? He knew what you were up to."

"They thought I was onto them," Fargo realized.

"They *knew* you were onto them," Daisy countered. "But you blew it, Fargo. You with your swelled head, thinking that you could take us on all by your lonesome. You really had your nerve tagging out after our wagons, I've got to give you that. But not much else. You're a fool, Fargo. If you wanted a run-in with us, you should have found yourself an army before you ever left Leavenworth. But it's too late now."

"Why?"

"Why?" Daisy exploded. She was venomous, she was angry. She was a pompous, incautious braggart, but she was also caught with her hair clenched in Myra's fist and a knife at her throat. Daisy was a predator ensnared in a trap, snapping and snarling, but she had to be more frightened than she let on.

"That's what I asked," Fargo said complacently.

"Why?" she repeated. "Because Harry's smarter than you, that's why. And he has twice as many men."

"So Harry is the brains behind Webster and McCormick?"

"You're damn right," Daisy asserted.

"And he's got eighty men, huh?" Fargo ventured, trying to look worried.

"More than eighty," she flaunted.

"Harry, smart?" Myra interjected. "Harry the brains behind anything? Now that is a laugh. Why, Daisy, that's almost as funny as you assuming that you have any intelligence."

"And what would you know, Myra? Harry's my man, not yours. And you were so gullible you never even knew it."

"Your man? What about Lilabeth?"

"Lilabeth's just a mark, no better than you. She owned that saloon and Harry needed it for an operating base. There was never any more to it than that."

"I don't know what you're bragging about," Fargo objected. "Seems to me you've all been duped by Harry. Leastways, I wouldn't leave a woman of mine sitting here with a knife at her throat."

"That shows what you know. I'm not supposed to be here. I was supposed to lure you out. But that Chatham never did do anything right. First, he runs off and then he can't accomplish a simple killing. And now Harry is going to be so mad."

"At you, though," Fargo reminded her. "Not at Chatham. Chatham's beyond all that."

"Yes, at me," she shouted. "And it's not fair. I blew up the wagon. I didn't have to do that. After all, Chatham only left that powder with me because he was scared of getting caught with it. And then that slimy, gutless bastard didn't get anything done. But I did. And Harry will just have to understand that when he comes for me."

"What makes you think he's coming for you?" Fargo asked. "Seems to me he's got a habit of using women. Look at poor Lilabeth. And even Myra, here. Hell, he even married Myra."

"He did not," Daisy spat. "Harry's my husband. He's always been my husband. We've been married nearly five years."

"How nice," Myra chirped. "That certainly lets me off the hook."

"Don't think you can bamboozle me, Myra. You wanted Harry, but you couldn't have him. Because he loves me. He's true to me."

"Good Lord," Myra snapped. "You sound just like Sally. What is all this hearts and romance and true-love nonsense? Have you lost your mind, Daisy? I've been with Harry. The man's a gigolo, an amorist, a sodomite, a rapist, and a pederast to boot. He's a depraved and twisted bully. Don't you read the papers? He saves his clippings. Woman beaten. Prostitute stabbed. Child murdered."

Myra had pulled the knife out of range, but she jerked Daisy's head back. "You can't tell me I'm the only one who knew why Harry saved those terrible things. After all, I tried to tell everyone for a while, until one of those someones actually listened. That poor man, he ended up as dead as all the people in those clippings. But you knew, didn't you? If you were married to him, you must have known."

"So what?" Daisy blazed. "And damn you, let go of me, Myra." Daisy pushed Myra's knife arm away with one hand as she tried to pull her hair out of Myra's grasp with the other. "I've had enough of your game," she railed. "Skye Fargo, namby-pamby that he is, is not going to let you kill me. So back off."

"You really are insane, aren't you, Daisy? And you're stupid, too. What ever gave you the idea that Skye Fargo could stop me from killing you?"

Myra whipped the knife back into place as she yanked on Daisy's hair so hard that it made Daisy fall backward into her lap. Then Myra bore down on the knife, pressing it into Daisy's throat, but with the blade sideways so the pressure merely cut off Daisy's air.

"Damn you, Fargo, stop her," Daisy rasped.

"Now, how is he going to do that, Daisy? Even if he shoots me, I'll still have time to slice your scrawny neck." Myra leaned down on the knife, choking Daisy.

Daisy gagged and her eyes protruded as though they would pop right out. One hand clawed at the air.

"For God's sakes, Myra," the Trailsman protested, taking a step toward them.

"Stay out of this, Fargo," Myra shot back.

Daisy's arms were both in the air, fingers clutching in a hopeless appeal. Her breath sounded like the creaking of a rusted hinge. "Skye," she rasped.

Daisy certainly put more faith in Fargo's virtue and ethics than he did. Truthfully, he halfway wished Myra had put an end to Daisy because he sure didn't like the idea of having Daisy back at camp.

"Contrary to what Daisy believes, I've got no interest in saving her. So do whatever you want, Myra," Fargo said as he skirted around the two women, circling wide so as not to arouse suspicion. But once behind them, he spun and lashed out with his boot, kicking Myra's forearm. The knife flew from Myra's hand.

Daisy was purple but still alive. Her hands flew to her throat as she curled off Myra's lap and into the dirt, coughing miserably.

Myra looked up at Fargo and sighed with blatant exasperation. "Oh, for God's sake, Mr. Fargo. I was never going to kill her, but she deserved a good scare."

"You'll pay for this, Myra," Daisy whispered hoarsely. "You'll pay when Harry comes."

"Won't we all?" Myra asked.

10

Despite the Indian menace, the land was peaceful. The sun had baked the prairie to a mellow gold here, where no trees rose, but an infinite variety of grasses rolled like a restless sea: bluegrass, redtop, switchgrass, wheatgrass, grama grass, needlegrass, and mostly little bluestem.

Out here in the thick of it, where hardly anyone ever bothered to go, the grasses grew shorter than to the east, and the skies spread wider. The little bluestem formed a fuzzy expanse just starting to turn to pinkish gold as it always did in August. But there were scattered clumps of other grasses, so that greener patches, taller grasses, and even bright-yellow sunflowers broke the monotony of endless waves of bluestem.

It was a comforting sort of place, much more suited to Fargo's temperament than a train boasting three dozen men, an inordinate number of beasts, and three too many women. He had left them behind three days ago after getting them through the burned area and concluding that Daisy wasn't planning any more explosive surprises.

He had ridden fast, pausing at Fort Kearny and Dobytown, but proceeding until he had found what he was looking for. There hadn't been any time to investigate where Harry's crew had been or exactly what they had been up to. But Fargo had picked up their tracks and he was pleased to be on their trail.

Poor Amos. Fargo couldn't help but feel a twinge of remorse at leaving him to cope with the innumerable problems aboard the train. There was Daisy, who was sullen and impossible, and determined to stir the men to passion and then goad them into fights. There was the constant threat of Indians.

There was Myra. Amos claimed she wouldn't cause any trouble. Fargo found that hard to believe; whenever she so much as spoke to him, she did her damnedest to be as irritating as nettles. And then, of course, there was sad-eyed Sally, who wouldn't cause Amos any problems but who looked at Fargo with such adoring intensity that it made him puff up like a strutting sage grouse, until guilt pricked at his conscience, which happened whenever he was around her for more than ten minutes.

Ridiculous birds sage grouse were, too, plumping up to twice their real size and clucking to impress some drab little hens. But the grouse were no more ridiculous than the way Fargo felt under Sally's beaming gaze. Sally's starry-eyed regard was often so rapturous that it made him check to see if he had acquired a halo or if he had merely forgotten to close his fly. If anything, Sally's admiration was a lot more bothersome than Myra's back talk. He was damn glad to be away from all of it.

Up ahead lay Webster and McCormick's train. It was an unusual operation, to say the least. Their tracks showed more than twenty times as many horses as Fargo's train. And horses attracted Indians the way manure drew flies. For a party out on the prairies this summer, dragging along too many horses was foolish. But, of course, the train had a lot of men, from the looks of it, even more than Daisy had gloated over, ninety or maybe a hundred.

Far more curious, however, were the two hundred or so mules they had—when all of their wagons were ox-drawn. Plus most of their wagons were empty. It was obvious from the tracks that there was no weight on them.

They were also herding several hundred head of cattle, a fair-sized flock of sheep, and even a couple dozen goats. It was plain that their game was rustling, and although Fargo didn't like to admit it, if the man called Harry was really the mastermind behind it all, he was a pretty clever scoundrel.

The train had swung south, away from the main trail and deep into Indian country. Daisy had indicated that Harry's men avoided hitting freight trains because such trains carried too many armed men, and in truth, the Indians felt much the same about the matter. A well-armed and well-trained party of teamsters could generally get anywhere without inordinate difficulty.

That didn't mean the Indians never attacked, but it did mean that trains were safer from attack, and they were almost certain to prevail even if they were attacked. If that hadn't been true, Fargo never would have brought a train out during this summer of upheaval. In all probability, Webster and McCormick's train was better-armed than most trains. So, in an odd way, the Indians were actually protecting those blackguards, since the soldiers were busy guarding the trail, and the local law, if there was any, wasn't equipped to fight Indians.

The country to the south was barren and progressively drier, but if a man knew his business, he could guide a train through it. Before Webster and McCormick's train got too near to civilization for comfort, they could divide their spoils into unrecognizable lots and herd some into Denver and some of them into New Mexico. Anything that was too well-branded, they could herd on over into Arizona, where the law was still a pretty loose proposition.

No wonder Daisy was so scornful. Only an idiot would be so taken with his own reputation that he would think he could stop such an operation by himself. Yet Daisy and Harry and Webster and McCormick and all the others had really believed Fargo meant to foil their scheme single-handedly.

Well, he thought, so be it. They were certainly going to be surprised when the army showed up, because he had no intention of wrangling with them himself. He had a train of his own to worry about.

But it wasn't going to be easy to get the army out here. So far this summer, the soldiers had blundered their way into an Indian uprising. Then they had gotten the trail closed. And now they had made it even more impassable by trying to open it again.

Back at Fort Kearny, the army was combining all the trains that got through into huge caravans, without even noticing that the resulting trains were so unwieldy that the wagon masters broke them up as soon as they were out of sight. The army was stretched thin just bungling all the problems they already had. They weren't going to be pleased when Fargo brought them another.

But Fargo felt confident that on the road ahead he would find plenty of reason for the cavalry to hasten to stop Webster and McCormick's scheme. He was only a day behind those thieves. They had passed only yesterday; the droppings in the road told him that.

Smoke fluttered on the horizon. The thin tendril of gray could be just a homestead cook fire, but this was a hellish hot day for baking. Fargo slowed the Ovaro to a plodding walk as he stared down intently at the welter of tracks. He focused his attention there, confident that the big pinto would let him know if any potential problems should appear on the horizon.

Following the tracks of Harry's train wasn't difficult. Not even an Apache could hide the movement of that many wagons and animals, and here they weren't even trying to be discreet. It was a blatant announcement that an army of freebooters had just passed through, with the confidence that they were so mean and numerous that nobody would dare perturb them.

After a quarter-mile, a side road appeared. It had seen recent heavy use, although it had not been built or maintained for much more than a wagon or two every couple of weeks. It was just a road to a farmhouse that couldn't be very far away. The road had ruts deep enough for dogs to hide in, and in the spring, some of smoother places would be axle-grabbing mud holes.

What kind of use had it seen in the past couple days? Fargo dismounted and examined the tracks. Three wagons, mule-drawn this time. Why mules when Harry's train was using oxen? Fargo decided to study on that later and looked closer, since if there was an answer, it had to lie right before him.

Examining sign was tedious, and just following the trail was often the least important part of tracking. By studying the sign, though, you could learn what kind of man or men you were after. Then you started trying to think like them, to figure out what they were up to, what they were after, where they had to go next. If you did that right, you could be there waiting.

On both sides of the meager road, as well as in the thoroughfare, there were so many animal tracks that it looked like a corral at first. The prints of split hooves meant cattle. They weren't shod, so they weren't wagon-pulling oxen, but part of someone's beef or dairy herd. The prints were lower in front, so the cattle hadn't just been ambling along; they were being driven at a fair clip. It looked as though a dozen or so cattle had passed.

There were prints of shod horses, too, all headed the same way—away from whatever lay at the far end of this road and toward the main route that Harry's main train had taken. Since the shoe prints were as big as platters and calked, they belonged to four draft horses that hadn't been pulling anything. There was also a set from a riding horse, which wasn't being ridden.

More interesting were the wagon tracks. They, too, were bound the same way, and the mule-drawn wagons had been heavily laden, because the iron tires had pressed deeply into the prairie dust. The wagons had been driven in a hurry, judging from how much the mules had churned up their part of the tracks. But why had the wagons gone hell-bent into ruts and potholes that any driver or mule would have avoided?

Because they couldn't see those jarring nuisances, Fargo decided. The trip had been made at night, under moonlight that allowed for general direction, but not for dodging specific obstructions.

So a bunch of livestock and three mule-drawn loaded wagons had come down this way last night. Had anything gone up this road? Sorting out tracks under tracks could take an eternity. But by staring hard and walking slow, Fargo found the outbound wagon tracks in a few spots. The outbound wagons had not been loaded.

Now that he knew what had passed here, Fargo turned his mind to why it had all happened. Three light wagons turn away from Harry's train. They return loaded, along with horses and cattle. There might be some kind of hidden supply cache out here, which would explain the wagons but not the livestock. A train with that many oxen wouldn't need to send out for beef.

Fargo pushed back the green feeling that started climbing in his throat. The only possible explanation was a nighthawk raid on a farmstead, which likely explained that wisp of smoke he'd seen earlier.

He lifted his eyes and the smoke was still there. Now that he had crested a small rise, he saw that there was a line of trees, indicating water, four or five miles away, and the smoke emerged from that general vicinity, although it was hard to be sure. This land dipped and rose a lot more than people thought.

Should he go back and follow Harry's caravan, or go on and see the scene of the raid?

The Trailsman knew he wouldn't like what he found at either place, so that wasn't a consideration. He walked back to the junction and debated flipping a coin. As he reached into his pocket, he saw some bootprints. Men had halted their wagons here and gathered to parley.

He identified four sets of boots, including one set that had walked away, up toward a rise about a hundred yards off, and had returned. So the men had reason to wonder about what was behind them. Maybe they were waiting for others who hadn't caught up to them, or maybe it was something else. Fargo decided he'd find why they had been curious, and spurred the Ovaro up the road.

After about five miles, when the road dropped toward the creek, Fargo slowed the big pinto to a walk. He turned a bend, and the farmhouse seemed to jump out in front of him, a house framed by the prairie grasses with a real lawn of its own, just a tiny patch of brilliant green, but lovingly tended. White clapboard and two stories, it was misplaced; it belonged outside a small town in Iowa.

A silver-maple sapling graced the yard, along with an elm, a pine tree, and a stand of corn. The house was tiny, almost a miniature of the real thing, but it must have cost its owner a pretty penny, the last real money he was ever likely to see because farming so far out wasn't a paying venture, not when every nail and board had to be hauled in. The poor bastard had to be quite a recluse—if he was still alive.

Fargo glanced back up at the roof. Shit. The smoke wasn't coming from the chimney; it was coming from the house. He threw caution to the wind and spurred the Ovaro to full speed.

"Anybody home?" he called, not bothering to knock as he opened the door.

There was nothing in the front parlor besides a pall of acrid smoke. No furniture, no rugs, no lamps, nothing, but there had been recently. Scrape marks showed where things had been pushed and dragged across the floor. Fargo turned and looked out the open door behind him. Until then, he hadn't noticed the wagon-wheel depressions in the tidy little lawn he had just raced over. Now, they were obvious, and Fargo lost all desire to see the rest of the house.

Harry's crew had taken everything of any value. There was no other explanation for the emptiness of the place. The furniture must have been pretty nice, too, considering the oak floor, the wallpaper, and the real glass panes in the windows—those things were about as common as whales in this part of the world.

Presuming that the owners of the place hadn't been real cooperative about letting Harry's raiders carry their belongings off, Fargo braced himself as he went into the next room, where he found what he expected.

The master of the house was on the floor, dead, and a lamp had been knocked over. Burning lamp oil had spread out to scorch the floor, but the oak was only smoldering. Scalped, disemboweled, and castrated, the home-owner was in much worse shape. Fargo knelt down beside the dead man.

The man had two bullet holes in his chest. The corpse looked awful, but the dying hadn't been so bad. The slashing had all happened after his death. But if the thieves had mutilated the man to make the murder look like the work of Indians, they had certainly done a poor job of it.

The scalping was messy and the resulting souvenir probably hadn't taken any prizes, since they had hacked rather than peeled the hair away. The rest of their work was just as gruesome, without any of the finesse Indians brought to the job.

Besides that, if Harry's boys had really wanted anyone to believe it was Indians, they wouldn't have taken the furniture. Indians didn't have much use for heavy furniture. What Indians liked were the things these men had left behind.

Odds and ends littered this room: papers, receipts, the shards of tossed-aside knickknacks, a toy horse, a cast-iron trivet with a picture of St. Louis blazoned on the ceramic hot plate, a framed sampler. Folks who didn't understand the Indians' preference for small decorative items didn't live a nomadic life. Fargo did. And he couldn't imagine Indians wanting a buffet or a set of dining-room chairs.

If Harry's men were always this sloppy about leaving evidence, Fargo figured the army was doing a much worse job than he had thought. And he hadn't given them much credit in the first place. Hell, the army should have figured out Harry's racket and arrested him long ago.

Fargo stood up and readied himself for the kitchen—a man didn't build a home like this unless he had a woman. The woman was Indian, or at least part Indian, but it was difficult to tell which, because her hair was gone and her face was badly swollen. Her clothes had been torn from her. They lay nearby, although the buttons were scattered everywhere.

Fargo turned away. He didn't want to examine the woman more closely. He already knew she had been raped, roughly, and more than once. That was obvious from across the room because of the way she had been left spread-eagled.

The Trailsman didn't want to look at her anymore, but he couldn't just wipe her image from his mind either. She had fought, she had lost, and so she had died even harder than her man had.

Upstairs, Fargo found two little boys. Neither one had been mutilated, but they hadn't fared any better than their parents. The smaller boy had been left on the floor, battered from head to toe. The boy had been raped, too, as had his brother on the bed. The older boy was black-haired and pretty small, maybe four or five. He was naked, with his face down and his rump up, torn and bloody.

Fargo headed for the stairs. The boy was dead and the bedclothes were stiff with blood. That was all Fargo needed to see. There wasn't anything he could do for these people. Besides, he wanted air.

The Trailsman had seen almost every kind of mangling the Indians could come up with, but none of it had ever seemed this bad. Maybe that was because the Indians didn't do things like this to their own kind. They did it to the enemy, be he Crow or Pawnee or white.

The folks in this house hadn't ever done anything to Harry's men; Harry and his friends only wanted their furniture and their livestock. They had to be insane, maniacal, twisted. Indians tortured to frighten their enemies, so what did Harry's men get out of it? Enjoyment?

Fargo slammed out the back door and headed for the creek. It wasn't a big creek, but it ran steady enough to give life to a few of the cottonwoods that ran along prairie rivers. He bent down to splash some water in his face, but stopped cold when he saw a bootprint. It was in damp sand, and it was frighteningly fresh.

The print hadn't been there for more than twenty minutes; the water pooling up into it was going to wash it away in another ten minutes. Fargo was suddenly very alert for strangers, but he knew from the gooseflesh tickling at his neck that he was already too late.

Someone was behind him. Fargo splashed some more water in his face, surreptitiously sliding one hand down for his boot knife as he did so. He slipped the knife up under the cuff of his flannel shirt, then stood.

"Hold it right there," a voice said as Fargo swiped at his face with his sleeve. "Put your hands up."

The Trailsman did as he was ordered, and turned around slowly. His assailant was young, sixteen or seventeen, not even a real man yet, but the boy was pointing a grown-up Colt at Fargo's heart.

"Hey, Clem, come see what I got me here," the boy shouted enthusiastically. "You're Skye Fargo, ain't you?"

"We've met?"

"Nope. But Harry's told us all what to look for. Hell, I'm going to get myself one fat reward for your scalp, that's for sure." The boy laughed gleefully. "Dammit, Clement," he shouted, "what in hell's keeping you?"

"Dammit yourself, Roy. I can't come now," a voice shouted back.

The boy laughed ribaldly. "Well, I guess I can let Clem finish up." He chuckled. "Since you ain't going anywhere."

"No," Fargo agreed calmly. "But you are." He looked beyond the boy. "Amos," he said quietly.

The boy turned his head and Fargo dived sideways,

throwing the knife simultaneously. The knife struck higher than the Trailsman had intended, burying itself to the hilt beside the boy's protruding Adam's apple. The kid was too damn young to be out here. He had fallen for the oldest trick in the book.

Roy dropped the Colt without firing a shot. The boy should have gone down instantly, but instead he stood with his hands clutching at his throat below the knife. His mouth flew open and blood and spittle oozed from the corner.

He was screaming, that's what he was doing, but his vocal cords had been severed.

Fargo had just drawn his Colt to stop the agony when, to his relief, the boy fell flat on his face.

Fargo looked for Clement. For a moment, he was amused to hear such familiarly rhythmic grunts, but then he remembered the boys in the upstairs bedroom. The Trailsman stepped from behind a cottonwood into a clearing edged by long brush.

What in hell was being partnered under Clement's bobbing ass? Fargo wondered as Clement's victim started to make noises like a dog with its tail caught in a door.

He fired. Clement was thrown sideways by the bullet, which passed through his skull. The shot was still ringing in Fargo's ears when he heard soft cries from the child who had skittered away from Clem's corpse.

The little body was quivering and the shoulders were shaking. The kid's head was curled down, and the knees were drawn up so that Fargo couldn't see anything but curved spine and quivering misery.

"Are you all right?" he asked.

The child didn't answer. Actually, the child was hardly making any noise at all. Its grief was silent, a lament of ragged breathing and palsied shivering.

Fargo wasn't at all sure what to do. He reached out and touched an angular shoulder blade.

The child came alive. She bolted up and lunged for the bushes. Her long hair tumbled down her back, and it was the first time Fargo knew he was dealing with a girl rather than a boy. He jumped up and went after her, catching her around the waist. She fought viciously, kicking and screaming and biting down hard on the arm he held her with.

"Easy, now. Easy," he shouted. "I'm not going to hurt you."

But she didn't stop fighting. He threw her over his shoulder and headed for the Ovaro. She was worse than Myra. Being so tiny, she could twist herself up better. She folded up and clamped her teeth into Fargo's shoulder.

When he got to the Ovaro, Fargo grabbed a blanket from a saddlebag and wrapped the naked little girl. Carefully, he set her on her feet, but she collapsed in a heap, sobbing woefully as if her world was over. Which it was. Everything she knew was back in that house— dead.

Fargo understood. His own folks had been murdered long ago. Thank God, he thought, it hadn't been like this. He crouched down beside her.

"Honey," he murmured, "I'm going to find some folks to look after you. That's what your mama would have wanted, isn't it?"

She regarded him suspiciously. She was definitely part-Indian. Her hair was a dark, wild tangle, and her face was thin, with well-defined cheekbones. She was a pretty little girl, but the most startling thing about her was her eyes, bright-blue eyes, the color of sky and water.

Fargo felt a surge of kinship. She would be all right, he decided. He would see to it.

11

Somehow the train had managed to get past the snarl at Fort Kearny. It was moving up the trail as Fargo rode in from the opposite direction, looking for Amos. Thick and gritty, the dust swirled into Fargo's nostrils and eyes. He pulled the blanket up over his passenger's face.

She was cradled in front of him on the saddle, asleep. Although travel had been awkward with a sleeping rider aboard, it had been easier than last night, when Fargo had lain awake for hours listening to her whimper.

Fargo saw Rogers. "Find Amos," he shouted, "and tell him we're going to take an early nooning. I've got some business to discuss. Pass the word to start pulling it over."

"Yes, sir," Rogers agreed.

Fargo pulled his bandanna up over his face and rode to the head of the train, where Amos found him as they had the wagons corralled. "What do you have there?" he asked as Fargo dismounted.

"A kid."

"A what?"

"Wake up now, honey," Fargo suggested.

First a brothel, then a child. At this rate, Fargo would soon be famous for packing along all the aggravations of home. He summoned a hand and told him to fetch the women. Then he stood the little girl carefully on her feet, tugging the blanket around her protectively.

"Why, it's Lucy," Amos exclaimed, slack-jawed.

"You know her?"

"Sure. Her mother's kind of a shirttail relation. Distant cousin to my wife."

"Her mother's dead."

"Mary?"

"If that was her name. They're all dead, except her." Fargo nodded at the girl.

Amos knelt in the dust in front of the child. "Lucy, do you remember me?" he asked.

Lucy burst into tears before throwing her arms around Winfield's neck.

Amos picked her up. "How?" he asked.

"Harry's men. Killed them all for their fine furniture. Amos, what in hell were those people doing way out there?"

Amos shrugged. "Wasn't so far out. Mary was half-Cheyenne. She visited with her family pretty often. Her mother. Her grandparents."

"But that house."

"Luke was homesick, I guess. He tried taking Mary and the kids back to Illinois. But it didn't work. Then she got homesick." Amos stood there absentmindedly stroking Lucy's hair. There was mourning in his eyes, a dazed and distant look.

"You were close to them?" Fargo asked.

Winfield brought himself back to awareness. He shook his head. "No. Luke was all East. I was all West. He came out here as an Indian agent seven or eight years back, I reckon. Mary must have been the only woman in these parts who could speak English. Her pa was a trapper. He abandoned her, her ma, and her brothers. Left them with their Cheyenne kin, but not before they all learned English. So Luke married her. Guess he loved her some. Surely loved the kids. But I don't think he was too happy trying to bring Illinois out here."

"You know of any relatives who would want the girl?"

"Her grandmother. But she's Cheyenne. Don't know

137

that Lucy should go to Cheyenne. Skye, I'm not sure there's any future in being Cheyenne."

"What about Luke's folks?"

"Don't know that they'd want her. Luke had a problem with being married to an Indian. I figure he picked up that shame from them."

The women strolled up just then, Daisy with them. When Fargo had sent for the women, he hadn't even thought of Daisy. She was, after all, under house arrest. Quite a ways off, her guard lounged against a wagon. Knowing Daisy, he probably needed the break.

Fargo fixed his gaze on Myra, since she was always mothering Sally. "I found a little girl on the trail. She needs tended to. I thought you could do it."

Myra put her hand to her breast and took a step backward. "A little girl? How little?"

"I think she's six," Amos volunteered. He gazed down at the top of Lucy's head. "Well, maybe not quite."

Myra glanced at Amos, who was still holding Lucy in his arms. The child clung to his shirt with clenched fists. Her face burrowed into his huge shoulder, and one skinny bare leg dangled down from beneath the blanket.

"Mr. Fargo, do I look like someone's mother?" Myra demanded, taking another step back.

"I didn't ask you to be her mother. I asked you to tend to her. She needs attention. She's been raped."

"Raped," Myra and Amos blurted at the same time.

"Yes, dammit. Tomorrow morning, I'll take her with me to Kearny. But I think somebody should see to her now."

"Well, I'm not going to do it," Myra said. "I don't know anything about children. If you want the child seen to, do it yourself."

"For God's sake, woman, be serious. The child's been raped. I can't see to her. She'd be scared to death."

"Well, what would you want me to do?" Myra

asked tentatively, casting an apprehensive glance Lucy's way.

"How in hell would I know?" Fargo balked.

Then he realized how truly frightened Myra looked. Daisy stood behind her, fairly smirking, while Sally stood to one side, staring over at Lucy and looking, as usual, as if she was about to cry. But then, so did Amos as he clasped the child and pondered her dark hair with worry in his eyes.

"Oh, hell," Fargo muttered, "I guess you could try talking to her. Find out if she hurts. Maybe you could look a little. See if she's bleeding."

"And if she is?" Myra asked in horror. "Oh, no, Mr. Fargo, I can't. I won't. She's a baby. I don't know anything about babies."

She spun away and ran off while Daisy burst into laughter.

"You get lost," Fargo ordered, turning on Daisy.

"Yes, sir," the woman jeered.

"Goddamm it, Myra," Fargo called, taking a step in Myra's direction.

"Wait," Sally cried. She put her hand on Fargo's arm. "I'll take care of the little girl if you'll let me."

Surprised, Fargo turned and stared down at Sally. "What would you do with her?" he asked suspiciously.

"Well, I'm no doctor. But what she needs most is somebody to hold her. And maybe help her wash and find her something to wear."

"Well, sure," Fargo agreed. "I guess you could do that."

Sally went over to Amos instantly, holding out her arms, and Amos handed Lucy over carefully. Lucy wasn't very big, but neither was Sally. Sally hoisted the child up on her shoulder and pressed her lips to the little girl's tangled hair. She glanced over at Fargo. "Thanks, Skye," she murmured.

Fargo watched Sally walk away with what suddenly looked like a heavy burden. "Thanks?" he said.

"Some women like children," Amos commented.

"Why did you think she was always mooning about getting married?"

"Guess I didn't think about it."

Amos nodded. "I wish I could say that. She's been nagging at me to tell all the men she's available."

Amos turned around and watched Sally, too. She was in clear sight, spreading out a bedroll in the shade of a wagon. Sitting down on it, she pulled Lucy onto her lap and began rocking back and forth. Sally sang, and the sound carried, just barely, a thread of a tune blending with the summer air.

"Don't know what to do about her," Amos said, turning back to Fargo. "The woman's surely got peculiar notions on how to gain a husband."

"You can say that again," Fargo agreed. "Amos, tomorrow morning I've got to go back to Kearny to report on Harry and his cohorts."

"I'd rather kill them with my bare hands," Amos said. His voice, always husky, was close to a growl.

Winfield's gentleness was gone. There was tension in him waiting to snap. There was tension in Fargo, too. He understood how Amos felt. But they had a train to run and Harry had at least ninety men.

"We could do it," Amos said.

"I'd like to," Fargo admitted. "But I've got other men to worry about. I've got a train, and I've got a contract with Sampson and Sons. This isn't their fight."

"Skye, what about Mary? Did they . . ."

"You don't want to know."

"Damn," Amos whispered. He folded his arms across his massive chest and stared off across the prairie.

Fargo didn't know what to say to him. Amos had known those people when they were alive. That was different from what the Trailsman felt—a sense of injustice, a sense of outrage, a sense that nobody should be able to get away with smashing a small boy into something almost unrecognizable. But the army would take care of Harry. It was the army's duty to take care of Harry.

"My wife died the same way," Amos announced gruffly.

Fargo had just given up on thinking of anything fit to say and had been about to walk away. He turned and stared at Amos. But Amos didn't look at him. He just gazed out at the grass, the sky, the vast sweep of land.

"Little more than a year ago," Amos continued softly. "The Cheyenne were doing poorly. No elk, no buffalo, no room. So I bought a little farm south of Denver. She hated it. Missed her folks, her sisters, the gossip, and what all. But I thought she'd get used to it. Until I went back after a trip and found her dead. Raped and beaten by white men. They killed my boy, too. Probably only meant to backhand him out of the way while they fooled with his mother, but he was little, only three."

"Amos, are you sure it was white men?"

"Had shod horses. Wore boots. Left cigar stubs and ashes all over the place. Didn't leave much else, though. Guess I'll never know who they were. Guess I'll never be able to find them."

"Amos, I'm sorry."

"What for? You're not as white as I am." Amos turned toward Skye with a cynical smile. There was something very frightening about that smile on the lips of such a huge, unpolished man. Winfield's red beard flowed to the middle of his chest, and his blond hair tumbled down over his shoulders.

Red Bear, Fargo thought, jolted as always at the association between Amos Winfield and the legendary Cheyenne killer.

Fargo spent the rest of the day with his attention fixed on the business of the train. He avoided talking to Amos, Sally, Lucy, Myra, Daisy, and even the men as he went about checking oxen, yokes, harness, hubs, and brakes. He listened as the wagons rolled, watched as the wheels turned, noted the gaits of the oxen, and observed the work of the men.

In spite of all the delays, they were making reasonably good progress on their journey to Denver. But it was time for him to start acting like a wagon master; women, children, dead folks, and Harry, they'd all been getting in the way of his job.

Fargo rose early the next morning. He had one more thing to do before he could get on with his work. He went to find Lucy.

Sally and the child were nestled together like sleeping kittens. They had kicked their light blanket aside, but they were decent. Sally wore one of her prim white nightgowns while Lucy was cloaked in one of Sally's blouses with the sleeves all rolled up. Sally's hair, which she normally kept tied back, was loose; it tumbled across both their faces, shielding their features from view.

"Sally," Fargo murmured, jiggling her shoulder.

Sally turned over and smiled at him sleepily.

"I've come for Lucy."

The smile disappeared. "Oh, Skye, do you have to take her? She's just getting settled after all those terrible things. Why can't she stay with me until Denver?"

"Sally, this is a freight train."

"I know, but . . ." Sally turned to embrace the child. "Oh, Skye."

"I know, Sally. But it's got to be done," he said sternly. "The sooner she's settled with new folks, the better."

Sally nodded solemnly as she sat up. "Lucy," she whispered, nudging the child's shoulder. "Lucy, Skye's here." Lucy opened her haunting blue eyes. "Remember what I told you, sweetheart?" Sally asked, gathering the little girl onto her lap. "Skye's going to take you to the fort, where there will be lots of soldiers to keep away the bad men. And there will be ladies, too, who will take care off you. And I'll bet they'll even find you a toy or two. Why, maybe even a doll or a little stuffed bear."

Fargo reached out to take Lucy, but she pressed herself to Sally and clung. "No," she shouted. "I don't want to."

"Come on, honey," Fargo prompted, stooping down in front of Sally to try to persuade the kid. "It'll be nice there."

"Nooooo," Lucy screamed.

Sally looked at him helplessly and he reached over and plucked the girl from Sally's lap. Lucy became a kicking, screeching savage once again, and Fargo held her at arm's length. She twisted and he dropped down, simultaneously pulling her backward onto his lap. Lucy howled; it was chilling, crazed, ear-piercing.

"Please, honey. It's all right," Fargo assured her. He held her tight, trying to restrain and comfort her at the same time. He raised one hand to stroke her cheek, and Lucy swooped at it. Bending abruptly, she chomped down on the back of his hand, sinking her teeth in deep.

"Goddamn," Fargo yelped, snatching his hand away.

But he had no sooner shifted than Lucy bobbed down, shot sideways, and scrambled for Sally. Sobbing hysterically, Lucy threw herself on the woman.

"Jesus," Fargo muttered, staring down at the bleeding little tooth holes in his hand.

"I guess I'll have to go with her," Sally said.

"Go with her?" Fargo considered the idea. "I suppose that would work. Besides, if you're looking for a man there are plenty at Kearny."

Sally nodded her agreement, but she didn't look enthusiastic.

"We have to figure out a story, though, some plausible explanation for why you were on a freight train. Hell, I know. We'll tell them you're Lucy's aunt. Tell them you were visiting your brother when the family was attacked. Tell them you managed to hide."

"Why?"

"Why? Because if you want a husband, you're going to have to explain what you were doing all those years you were whoring. And if you're Lucy's aunt, you can keep track of her and make sure they do right by her."

"Oh, no, Skye, I can't do that. I can't lie. If somebody does marry me, it wouldn't be fair."

143

"Fair? Since when is any woman fair?" Fargo demanded. "Dammit, Sally, soldiers don't marry whores. You say you want a husband. Well, then, you're going to have to lie."

"I can't, Skye. I've got to tell the truth. After all, what if one of those soldiers married me and found out the truth later? I couldn't let that happen. I guess I'll just have to take my chances with honesty."

"Are you crazy? You tell them you've been a whore, they'll put you over with the camp followers. Armies have rules about such things. You think they just let whores wander the halls and hang out in the men's rooms? How are you going to watch over Lucy if they've stuck you off with the whores?"

"Is that all you care about?"

"Well, of course not, but . . ." Fargo felt embarrassed. He didn't know whether Lucy was all he cared about, but she was definitely the only one whose welfare he had really thought about. All that had registered when Sally had mentioned leaving was relief. And he figured he had probably been far too transparent about that. "Sally, I'm sorry."

"No, I'm sorry," she sniffed. "You're right. Lucy's more important. I don't know what got into me, Skye. Nobody would ever want to marry me anyway."

"Oh, for God's sake, Sally, don't be ridiculous," Fargo said as he stood up and brushed off his pants. Pausing in midswipe, he stared down at Sally.

She was sitting cross-legged, her chin on the top of Lucy's head and her arms wrapped around the child's skinny body. Sally's hair was everywhere, framing the two of them in a picture of maternal harmony.

"Somebody will marry you," Fargo told her, knowing it was true. No matter what she had been, Sally had that look—pretty, sweet, gentle. Just seeing her made a man yearn for hearth and home, even if he had been drifting so long he couldn't rightly remember what those things were like. Even if he usually craved those things about as often as he hankered after French champagne.

"I don't know," Sally mumbled.

"Oh, hell, of course somebody will. Why, just yesterday Amos told me he wouldn't mind marrying you."

"He did?" she piped eagerly.

"Sure."

"Do you think he really means it? Do you think he really might?"

"Sally, I didn't mean it that way," Fargo protested. "He was just saying if he was me, he would marry you."

"Oh," Sally whispered, gazing up at Fargo with a puzzled look on her face. "But not if he was him?"

"Well, no," Fargo said. "Look, I guess I'll make better time riding to Kearny by myself. So we'll just have to figure out something for you and Lucy in Denver. All right?"

She agreed and Fargo walked away.

He was just mounted on his Ovaro and almost gone when Myra came running.

"Mr. Fargo, wait," she called.

"Oh, damn," he groaned.

Myra looked nervous, fluttery, and unsure of herself, which wasn't like her at all. She stood there looking up at him, a very pretty woman who clearly didn't have lust on her mind. She looked almost as mournful as Amos.

"Mr. Fargo," she said, then hesitated.

"Well, what?"

"Well, ah . . ." She licked her lips.

"Ah?" he prodded.

"Yes, well, I, ah . . ."

"Well, get on with it, woman, before my horse retires. Horses don't live as long as people, you know."

"Well, Mr. Fargo, it's just that I feel I owe you an apology," Myra gushed hastily. "Amos pointed out that I've been very rude and disrespectful, and upon reflection I have to admit that that is true. Amos said he thought it was because you look so much like Harry. I suppose that might be true, too. But, of course, that's not a very good excuse for my behavior."

"Do I really look like Harry?"

"Well, yes, I think so," Myra said.

Fargo didn't know why that bothered him. Ordinarily something like that wouldn't have bothered him. But his mind flashed back to Lucy's house. To Lucy's mother. To Lucy's brothers, so obviously raped. And to Roy, that jug-eared bastard who kept squawking while he clutched at his throat. And to Clement, who was as pale and pink-eyed as a white rat. Fargo's mind reeled with distaste.

"Well, are my apologies accepted?" Myra demanded.

"Oh, sure," Fargo allowed. "Except the worst thing you ever said to me was that I looked like Harry."

12

"Mr. Fargo, we can't go chasing after every dubious story we hear. We have a fort to defend."

"Dubious?" Fargo glared at the lieutenant sitting across from him. Fargo felt like grabbing the man, but the lieutenant's desk intervened.

Fort Kearny was overrun with backed-up trains and fleeing settlers, so no one who knew anything was available. Fargo had gotten stuck with this pompous jackass who thought he knew everything. Thirtyish, negligently handsome, and cocky, the lieutenant leaned back in his chair, twirled a pencil, and paid more attention to it than he did to Fargo's story.

"Yes, dubious. Even you must see that your story does have conflicting elements. You yourself admit that the man and his wife were scalped and mutilated, which is consistent with Indian tactics."

"I told you who did it."

"And you were there when they perpetrated those atrocities?"

"Of course not, but—"

"Mr. Fargo, I cannot allow you to disrupt the running of Fort Kearny with half-baked tales. There's an Indian war going on. We have important matters to pursue."

"Then why aren't you pursuing them?"

"Mr. Fargo, I am sure you are sincere, but you are dangerously deluded. We at the fort have noted that the Indians have changed their methods this summer and that they are using wagons more frequently. But it's only to be expected that Indians will take advantage of the white man's superior technology."

147

"Indians aren't using wagons," Fargo protested. "Harry's using wagons. And what in hell kind of advantage is there to wagons out where there aren't any roads? Or do you think the Indians are out there clearing and leveling roads, too?"

Studying his pencil intently, the lieutenant raised one eyebrow and sighed. "Mr. Fargo, you are being insubordinate. I am an officer."

"Insubordinate?" Fargo blasted. "I can't be insubordinate. I'm not even in the military. I'm being insulted, that's what I'm being. Goddammit, would you put that pencil down and listen?" Fargo leaned over the lieutenant's desk and snatched the offending object from the man's grasp. He tossed it back over his shoulder, and the lieutenant jumped to his feet.

"If you continue this behavior, sir, I will have you arrested for assaulting an officer."

"Assaulting? Do you even know what assault is?" Fargo stomped toward the door and the lieutenant was on his heels. The Trailsman spun around and glared down at the uniformed little weasel. "Do you want to see an assault?" he demanded.

The officer stepped back.

"Then go out and see Harry's men at work," Fargo railed. "Now, that's assault. And I'm going to find somebody in this godforsaken hole who can help me stop it."

Realizing that Fargo wasn't planning to wallop him, the lieutenant recovered his courage. He stepped briskly around Fargo and grasped the doorknob with one hand. Then, confident that his mode of escape was assured, the lieutenant got downright nasty.

"Mr. Fargo, I cannot allow you to wander around here causing dissension. Therefore, I'm afraid I'm going to have to detain you. It will, of course, be a temporary measure, since I am quite sure your temper will have cooled by the time the commander returns next week. At that time you can take your grievance up with him."

"You think you're going to have me arrested?"

"Yes."

Fargo planted a left hook squarely under the officer's jaw. Fool that he was, the lieutenant stood there for an instant looking dumbfounded, until he crumpled.

"Damn," Fargo muttered. Grasping the lieutenant under the arms, he pulled him out of the doorway. Then he moved through the hall hastily. Once out of the building, he fairly flew. He was on his horse and a mile from Fort Kearny before five minutes had passed.

He couldn't afford to squander five or six days in the stockade at Fort Kearny. Perhaps once the commander returned, Fargo could straighten the mess out, but for now he had cut off all hope of aid from Kearny.

He raced west toward his waiting train. The pinto's hooves thundered and the dust spumed out behind. Harry was out there doing God knows what to God knows who. He had to do something to stop him, and there wasn't any time to waste.

As soon as Fargo reached his train, he hunted down Rogers. Webster and McCormick's train was headed straight into the Colorado Territory, so Fargo told the former Pony Express rider everything he knew about Harry's work, sparing no details. He let the images surge and pour from him as he tried to make Rogers see what he had seen.

"Jesus, Mr. Fargo, why would anybody do something like that?"

"Who knows why? All I know is we've got to stop them. I've met the commander at Kearny and we'll never get help from them. But the governor of Colorado Territory commands a militia."

Rogers nodded. He looked sick and Fargo wondered if he had overdone it. But there was no overdoing it. Rogers had to understand the nature of these men. He had to be able to communicate it.

"How soon do you think you can get to Denver? I'll give you money to buy fresh mounts where you can find them, and Amos can tell you about every ranch along the way that might supply horses."

"Well, if I can leave within the hour . . ."

Fargo nodded his encouragement.

"And I do manage to get mounts, and I can get in to see the governor right away, I could be back in five days."

"Let's do it."

Fargo already knew it was going to be the longest five days in his life. He wasn't made for waiting, but he had little choice. He would have preferred to go himself, but he had a job to do here. Rogers was a good man, and he could ride.

Within the hour, Rogers was gone, and Fargo was back at his work, walking along beside the oxen, sweating in the heat, and squinting at the dust. He surely didn't know why some men thought this was exciting. By the time they got the train pulled over that evening, Fargo felt as if he had rolled in a mud puddle and let it dry on him.

Fargo washed, changed, rinsed out his pants and shirt, and went for a walk. He wanted to be alone, but when he rounded a wagon to avoid an impending encounter with a group of sociable teamsters, he ran right into Sally. Lucy was with her.

"Skye, you're back. Have you heard the news?"

"What news?"

"I did what you told me," Sally gushed. "I asked Amos and he said yes."

"He said yes to what?"

"To marrying me. And we're going to keep Lucy, too." Sally reached down and ruffled the child's hair. "Isn't it wonderful, Skye? Why, I still can't believe it. Amos is such an important man, and he's been a wagon master and everything. And he has a farm too, and he doesn't drink hard or anything. And he's even nice."

It wasn't dark yet, the sky was still lit by the blue twilight of late summer. Sally's eyes were lit, too. Her cheeks were glowing and her face was radiant. She clung to Lucy's hand while the little girl burrowed into her skirts, hiding her face from Fargo.

"Do you know what else Amos said?" Sally ran on. "He doesn't want to be a freighter anymore. Amos actually said he'd stay home with me and Lucy. He even said he didn't want to hear one more thing about other women. Oh, Skye, Amos told me that once he was married, he wouldn't want any other women. Why, he said if I didn't mind his carousing, he would wring my neck. Amos told me that not minding was unnatural, that women were supposed to mind."

Tears rolled down Sally's cheeks. She was the cryingest woman Fargo had ever met. There had to be deep reservoirs behind her eyes to keep all those tears flowing.

"Oh, Skye," she whispered reverently. "Amos wants a real marriage. I'll be a real wife."

Fargo nodded. He didn't have the heart to burst Sally's bubble, but it was crazy. Amos couldn't marry her just because she was asking.

"Sally, where is Amos?"

"He went to scout along the river to find a good site for the nooning tomorrow. But you knew that, Skye. You sent him. You said the oxen had to be well-watered because there were alkali holes ahead."

"Oh, sure, I remember," Fargo said, relieved that he wouldn't have to face Amos tonight.

Lucy peeked out from behind Sally's skirt and smiled shyly before hiding her face once again.

"She looks good," Fargo commented.

"She's doing fine," Sally agreed, turning to pick the child up.

Sally swung Lucy onto her shoulder and the girl cast Fargo a triumphant grin before she pressed her face against Sally's neck. "We're all doing fine."

"That's nice," Fargo said. "But I've got some things to take care of." He hurried away.

The awkward moments in his life were building into a steady stream, and he was already flustered enough. He craved action. Feeling as nervous as a caged cat, he paced outside the corralled wagons. He hated waiting, and he still had almost five days of it ahead of him.

"Mr. Fargo?"

He whirled around. "What in hell? For God's sake, don't sneak up on me, woman."

"I'm sorry," Myra said. "But I heard you sent Rogers to request the aid of Governor Evans."

"I did."

"Do you think the governor will respond?"

"How in hell would I know? But it's the man's duty to respond."

"Then you think he will?"

"Not necessarily. After all, it was the army's duty to respond, too. And what in hell am I supposed to do if Evans doesn't respond?" Fargo asked, loosing some of his vexation on Myra, who surely deserved it after all the trouble she'd given him. "I can't just leave Harry and his crew to gallivant around cutting up women and children. But I don't have the men to fight him."

"But if Governor Evans won't send someone, you'll have to fight Harry yourself."

"Dammit, Myra. Don't you think I've thought of that? But I can't do it. My men are teamsters, not soldiers. They're facing enough risk just getting this train to Denver. Maybe they would be willing to fight Harry, but I've only got thirty-six men, thirty-seven counting me, and he's got ninety or more. At best, half of my men would be killed in a fight with Harry—if we were lucky, and if we won."

"So there's a chance dear Harry is going to get away with murder—again." She sighed. "And again, and again, and again."

"No, I won't let him."

"Don't be silly, Mr. Fargo. There's very little one person can do. One person can't even get others to listen."

"This has gotten personal with me. I'll stop him," Fargo vowed.

"Mr. Fargo, Harry's not worth dying for."

"Really? Then why are so many people doing it?"

Fargo started to pace again. He couldn't seem to stand still, and yet that was all he was really doing, while Harry was out there . . .

"Mr. Fargo, you need to loosen up," Myra announced as she came up behind him and put her fingers on his shoulders. Her thumbs pressed into the ache growing between his shoulder blades. "I know how frustrating it gets to hate Harry and be unable to do anything about it." She paused as her thumbs seemed to erase Fargo's soreness. "But he does have a way of showing people that life is short and not to be wasted."

Myra's hands moved down to the small of his back. Her deft palms kneaded Fargo's weary muscles. "I can give you a great massage," she whispered. Her lips were just inches from Fargo's ear; she stood almost as tall as he did. "There were Chinese doctors in San Francisco."

Fargo bristled. "I know what those Chinese doctors use for relaxing folks—opium. I don't need any of that or any more of your special herb treatments."

It seemed strange, and Fargo had to shake his head and turn a bit to be sure. But it was true. Myra, the loudest harpy he had ever met, was giggling.

"Not all Chinese doctors," she murmured between titters. "Many of them have a theory that the body has pressure points. If you apply pressure to the right place, it relieves the pain somewhere else."

Fargo mulled for a moment. His own tension seemed to be vanishing into Myra's hands as they soothed his back. "I've heard of that," he conceded. "And you know where those places are on a body?"

Myra's arms slipped around his waist and her hands found his groin. Fargo felt new tension rising against his fly, and so did she. Her limber fingers pressed in response to his pressure.

Her tongue lapped at his right earlobe for a moment before she spoke. "I know the most important place on your body right now. Perhaps we should go somewhere so I can work on it."

Fargo reluctantly paid some heed to his surroundings. They were beside a wagon, outside the circle formation, where a fire began to grow as men relaxed. Fargo grudgingly recalled that he hadn't spread his bedroll yet.

Myra was pressed so close against his back that he could feel her nipples rising against his shoulder blades. She seemed able to sense his consternation and its cause. Wordlessly, she sidled around him. And now it wasn't her hands that were rubbing through his button fly. It was her own pressure point, insistently grinding against his, as her hands moved back up to his shoulders and she planted a kiss.

Fargo was of no mind to argue, not even when she started tugging his tongue out by its roots while experimenting with interesting new ways to arrange her lips against his. When he caught his breath, he knew that the time it would take to find and spread his bedroll would seem like eternity.

She sensed his agitation, eased back a bit, and started lifting her frock, her action visible in the flickers that filtered below and between the wagons.

"Dammit, woman, there's a time and a place for everything," Fargo protested softly.

"I know, Skye, I know." Myra tossed the frock over her shoulders. Above her thin waist and lust-glistened thatch, her bobbing full breasts seemed to emphasize her words. "There is a time and place for everything. For this, it's now and here." She stepped forward with a wanton look that might have scared any man less experienced and less eager than the Trailsman.

His shirt came off faster than he had thought possible, but even so, Myra had his trousers down before he reached the last button. He stepped out of his boots and clothes. He briefly thought about pulling off his socks, but what the hell. Myra still had her knee-length stockings on, and the ground here was a bit rough for going barefoot.

The prairie was also too rough for rolling around on. But Myra had the same idea as the Trailsman. Stay on your feet. She rose, pausing at the tip of his shaft for a lingering kiss while her breasts played soothingly against his thighs. Fargo's fingers instinctively kneaded her surprisingly soft shoulders as tendrils of her blond hair played against the backs of her hands.

His intensity grew as her mouth lingered. He knew she had other plans, though, because he felt her pull back, getting in one last lick before her body rose and her eyes met his.

She smiled as she pressed her torso against his and arched her back rearward a bit, so that he might enjoy seeing the roundness of her full breasts. "Skye, I've never done it quite this way before," she confessed.

Fargo didn't pause to try remembering. His tool seemed to have a will of its own as she shifted a bit, and it navigated to the right spot. Warm delight surrounded the prow and he began to rock, his hands enjoying the responsiveness of Myra's rump.

With her head cocked back and her face aimed at the stars, Myra let off a shrill wail that would have shamed a lonesome coyote. Fargo thought to lean forward, perhaps smother the sound with a kiss, but that would mean losing some of that connection below, and that was the last thing in the world he wanted to lose any of right now.

Instinctively, he glanced around furtively, wondering if any of those flitting shadows resulted from spectators rather than the flickering of the fire. Then, with another banshee howl, Myra arched back even more and engulfed him. He bent his knees for better thrust and plunged in deeper.

Fargo was beyond caring what sort of attention Myra's vocal ecstasy might attract. There was no longer a world around him. Just Myra, head back, breasts aimed at him, thighs trembling, providing an ever-deeper harbor for his relentless pulsing energy.

When he exploded deep within her, she let loose with an ear-shattering scream that spanned at least four octaves while her internal muscles moved up and down his scale. Since Fargo had a firm grip on her splendid rump, she kicked loose somewhere in there, and when the passion settled a bit, her kneecaps were jammed into his armpits.

Fargo heard something and glanced over his shoulder. It was Sinclair, on night guard and keeping a polite distance as he stood between wagons. Fargo didn't know whether to feel embarrassed or relieved because his night guards were doing their work.

"Sinclair," Fargo muttered while Myra continued to wrap herself around him in interesting ways.

"Mr. Fargo, I didn't watch. Honest. And I kept the others away . . ." At Fargo's grunt, his words came out faster. "But I did want to tell you that I went ahead and spread your bedroll, over to the other side in a dip that's a bit more private."

"Let's go try that." Myra giggled.

"You ain't mad at me, are you, Mr. Fargo?" Sinclair sounded a lot more worried than his boss was.

"Not unless you neglect to pick up our clothes and toss them over there in a little while." Fargo started laughing, for the first time in what seemed like months. Myra sure did know how to release a man's tension, and by the time they made it to the bedroll, they were both ready to find more ways to release it.

By dawn, Fargo was feeling wearier, but more relaxed. He rolled out of his bedroll and groaned. Myra had taken some of his aches away, but she had added new ones.

He stood for a moment, staring down at her, a very pretty woman who had found a way to keep his dark thoughts at bay. He was more than grateful.

It was gray dawn, quiet, though it wouldn't be for long. Fargo left Myra to sleep while she could, before the men and animals made a ruckus of the morning. He went to find Amos.

But he found Sally instead. She was between the wagons, with her bare legs twined around a man's waist. The man was standing, but leaning far over her, nuzzling at her neck while she giggled breathily. Her body was arched, her head was back, and her hair was trailing nearly to the ground. It was a ludicrously precarious position, and if they both kept on laughing the way they were, they were going to tumble right over.

Fargo felt incensed. Lucy was sleeping right around

the wagon's corner, and Sally was an engaged woman. He wasn't exactly sure what Sally and her friend were doing. Her nightgown was up around her thighs, but the man was fully clad. On the other hand, if the man's pants were open . . .

"Sally," Fargo blared.

Sally gasped and her shoulders swung up while her legs swung down. Instantly, the man lifted her off him and whirled around so that his back was toward Fargo as he made himself decent. The little lift had shown Fargo exactly what the two of them had been doing.

"Skye," Sally murmured, her cheeks flaming.

The man straightened and turned. And Fargo gawked. It was Amos. By God, it really was Amos, although the Trailsman had never seen such a transformation before in his entire life.

"You look different," Fargo said. Winfield looked embarrassed, that's how he looked, and suddenly Fargo felt ridiculous for having disturbed them.

Amos rubbed his cheek with his knuckles. "Thought I'd clean up a little for Sally. Thought she might like it."

The beard was gone, the long hair was clipped, and he wore ordinary clothing, no trailing rawhide, no beads, no elk-tooth geegaws. If it wasn't for Winfield's sheer mass, Fargo never would have recognized him.

Who would have believed that under all that hair, Amos had hid a face as purely wholesome as Sally's? His jaw was squarish and there was a cleft in his chin. But the most remarkable thing was how young he looked. Together, they looked like two kids caught behind the barn.

"Sally, I think maybe Skye wants to talk to me privately," Amos suggested.

Sally reached out to touch Amos. Her small hand glided down Winfield's massive chest as she cast a timid glance at Fargo before hurrying away.

It was another of those awkward moments, and Fargo had nothing to say.

"You needed to see me?" Amos asked.

"No, not really," Fargo answered. Then he stalked off, leaving Amos to think whatever it was Amos would think about his embarrassing intrusion.

If Amos was willing to marry Sally just because she was asking, then let him, Fargo thought. It wasn't anybody's business, and maybe they would even be happy, he decided as the waiting began again. It accompanied Fargo through a day of toil.

Fortunately, Myra was just as addicted to action as Fargo was. He awoke abruptly, jolted out of a vicious nightmare. And he knew Harry was out there, doing something to someone, right then, and there was nobody to stop him.

Resigned to try more pacing, Fargo sat up and felt around for his pants, but Myra was next to him. Her hand slipped along his bare backbone.

"Skye, it's all right," she whispered, drawing him back down.

He sighed as her hands went to work on him. Within minutes, Myra was breathing raggedly. And although it wasn't the first time that evening, nor the second, or even the third, Fargo rolled on top of her with driving urgency as she opened herself to him, offering forgetfulness.

The camp came alive. Somebody shouted, another man answered, and then everybody got in on the din, men, oxen, and horses alike.

"What in hell?" Fargo murmured, pushing himself up off of the breasts he had been recuperating on.

He searched for his pants again and Myra sat up. Then Fargo stood up and she screamed. Leaping up behind him, Myra threw her arms around his waist and tried to push him aside.

"Skye, watch out," she warned.

A gun boomed and Myra gasped, sagging against him. Fargo reeled but he couldn't catch her before she crumpled onto the bedroll. He dropped down beside her, but before he could do anything, he saw a blur of movement.

Somebody was standing in the shadow of the closest

158

wagon, and Fargo was presenting an excellent target, bathed as he was in moonlight. Instinctively, he launched himself toward the wagons and the shade. He made it to the darkness in a headlong plunge, but he didn't have his Colt, his boot knife, his belt knife, or his Sharps. He didn't even have his pants.

"Over here," he shouted, pitching sideways to avoid the bullet he thought would follow. But the camp was awake and some of his men were certain to hear him. "Here," he called again, rolling over in the dust. He scrambled away from the sound of his own voice until he came to rest in the dirt under a wagon, where it was as black as pitch.

Fairly sure that his gun-carrying assailant couldn't see him, Fargo scooted around in a half-circle, praying that his movement wouldn't be detected. Slowly, he inched around until he could peer out at his moonlit campsite, and shock washed over him like ice water.

None of his men had come this way yet, but someone was standing over Myra with a gun pointed at her head. For all Fargo knew, Myra was already dead, but it didn't matter. He couldn't let the intruder shoot her.

Without thinking twice, Fargo plummeted from his hiding place, howling his outrage as he dashed straight toward the armed invader. A shot boomed, then another, and the assailant fell.

While Fargo just stood there feeling astounded, men came running from all directions. He stared at the body sprawled across his bedroll. "Who fired the shots?" he asked, turning to his men.

They all just looked at him blankly.

A whisper rose from the body of the fallen gunman. "Help."

"Why, he's not dead," one of the men said.

"Help."

Suddenly understanding, Fargo dashed over to pull the body off Myra. "Myra, are you all right?" he asked.

"No," she answered lowly.

Fargo's eyes swept across the woman's slender body,

pausing at the little derringer she clutched in her hand. Myra had fired the two shots; she had saved him. Her skin glowed in the moonlight, but there was blood everywhere, making dark smudges upon her moonlit flesh.

"Where?" Fargo demanded, crouching over her and taking her face in his hands. "Where, Myra?" The panic assailed him, a panic he had never felt when there was merely a gun leveled at his gut.

"Oh, Skye," she whispered, smiling, although not very convincingly. She was in pain; it was obvious. Her features were too rigid, her jaw was set. "I'm all right," she said hoarsely, the words slurring between her clenched teeth. "Daisy never did do anything right."

"Daisy?"

"Of course, Daisy. Who else would want to kill us? But it's only my ass, Skye. Yet . . . Oh, God, it hurts."

"Myra, tell me where it hurts. Are you sure she didn't hit anything important?"

Myra gazed up at him. "And I always thought my ass was important," she whispered, and then she laughed, but it didn't sit right with her. "Help me turn over," she shouted suddenly. "My ass is on fire, and here I am resting on it."

Fargo hastened to comply, and sure enough that was what was wrong with Myra. A wicked crease ran all the way across her bottom. It was darker than the smudges, a deep well of blood, but it was only a flesh wound.

"Jesus, I was scared it was something vital," Fargo muttered with relief.

"It is vital," Myra snapped.

And Fargo started to laugh.

"Oh, God, don't make me laugh again," Myra groaned. "It makes everything jiggle."

At that, all of the men laughed, and Fargo looked up and realized that he and Myra were both absolutely naked with a whole trainload of men gaping at them. "Break it up," he ordered. "You're dismissed. No, wait. Is that really Daisy?"

One of the men stooped over the body. "It is."

"And?"

"She's dead."

"What happened? How did she shake her guard? Where did she get the men's clothing?"

"Well, sir, her and Sinclair, they, ah . . . She, er . . . Well, meaning no disrespect sir, but I think they were doing what you were doing, when Daisy cracked Sinclair over the head with a rock. Then Jameson heard him moaning and he called out an alarm."

"Is Sinclair all right?"

"Yes, sir, he's got a headache, but he's fine. 'Cept he might think twice before ever enjoying himself again."

He should have thought before trying it the first time, but Fargo hadn't exactly been setting a good example. He stayed silent.

"Don't be silly," Myra chafed. "I'm not going to let it stop me."

Daisy, bless her dear departed soul, had taken the edge off Fargo's restlessness. As soon as Myra was properly stitched and bandaged, Fargo fell into a deep dreamless sleep. But three nights later he was fretting again.

"Oh, Skye," Myra said, "I can't stand just waiting and thinking. There must be something we can do."

She lay on her stomach on his bedroll while he sat nearby leaning against a storage box and smoking a cigar.

"We could talk, I suppose."

"That's all?" She raised her head and grimaced at him.

"Yes. I figure that's all, leastways that's all if you prize that ass of yours as much as I do." Fargo held out his cigar and studied the glowing tip. "Myra, I've been wondering about Sally and Amos. What do you think will become of them?"

"Skye, I know what will become of them. They'll milk cows, raise chickens, and plow fields. Amos will be so bored, he'll fall asleep before seven every night.

Sally will gain twenty pounds. And together they'll produce a passel of whiny children to drool all over both of them."

"Then you don't think they'll be happy?"

"Of course they'll be happy. That's what they think happiness is."

A commotion arose. A man came running. "Mr. Fargo," he shouted, "it's Rogers."

The Trailsman was there in a flash. Rogers looked terrible. "I didn't expect you till tomorrow," Fargo said.

"Mr. Fargo, I'm sorry. They wouldn't listen. I couldn't make them listen. Evans had this man with him, a Colonel Chivington. He kept going on about how Lucy and her folks weren't really white, about how they were Indians, about how her and her brothers would have grown up Indians, about how nits make lice and other strange stuff. Then, after all that, he said savages had gotten those folks because white men wouldn't do such things. Mr. Fargo, this Chivington bastard, he believed me. He believed it was white men, I know he did. But he wouldn't admit it because Lucy and her brothers were Indians. I'm sorry."

"You did your best," Fargo said, turning away.

But Winfield grabbed his arm. "They turned you down," he said flatly.

"Dammit, Amos," Fargo bristled. "I know you want to go after Harry. I want it too. But I won't risk my train, we can't do it alone and nobody will help."

"You only tried one side. Why don't we try the other side?"

"What other side?"

"The Indians. I bet they don't appreciate Harry wandering around committing depredations in their name. So why don't we ask them?"

"How?"

"I'll take care of it."

"Amos, are you sure they won't just kill you?" Fargo asked.

But Amos was gone. The huge man had evaporated

into the dusk like smoke, and Fargo thought he'd been left to wait—again. Except Amos returned within five minutes.

"All right, let's go," he said. "I've sent word. They're waiting."

"Waiting?"

"Uh huh."

"You had this planned," Fargo accused. "Why didn't you tell me?"

"Didn't think you'd go along with it unless it was necessary."

The sun was dipping into the west the next day when Amos and Fargo arrived at the great Indian camp. They had just crested a rise when Fargo reined the Ovaro to a halt and gazed at the gathering of warriors below. Scattered across the plain were more than five hundred tepees, decorated in the colors and emblems of the Arapaho, Cheyenne, and Sioux tribes.

"Why the Arapaho and Sioux?" Fargo asked.

Amos shrugged as if the answer was obvious. "Harry and his men have been causing trouble for all the tribes. The army doesn't pay much attention to whether a red man is Cheyenne, Cherokee, or Apache. If some Indians are causing trouble, all the Indians take the blame these tribes have suffered and they want revenge."

Fargo nodded. There were other questions he had, questions about how Amos had arranged all this. They turned inside his head, but he held his peace. This gathering would get a job done, and that was what was important.

They rode down the rise and into camp. Amos was wearing the amulets of his people, and clearly the two white men were expected. Yet Fargo was still nervous entering the armed camp of nearly one thousand warriors. Many of the fierce-looking braves stared intently at the Trailsman, and he wondered if any of them would attempt to challenge him here. It would not be good to have to defeat an ambitious buck, and it would be worse to lose.

But Amos' bearing and reputation served to discourage any brawls. He was massive in the saddle and already more ferocious-looking than Fargo had ever seen him. His jaw was set and in his eyes there burned a low, constant fire. It was easy now to picture him as Red Bear.

They rode to near the center of the camp, to a tepee bearing Cheyenne designs. From the greetings Amos received, it was clear that this place had been reserved for him. It was also clear that there was little for Fargo to do until the next morning, when the attack would take place. Amos explained that he would work his way through the camp, meeting with the leaders and encouraging the warriors. But for Fargo, it was best that he remain here. There was no point in taking the chance that a young brave might decide to eliminate one more of the white men who were stealing their land.

"We'll ride out just after dawn," Amos revealed. "Harry and his men are about an hour to the southwest. The scouts report that they aren't running a disciplined group; they get up late and are slow to start moving. We should have no problem taking them by surprise."

As Winfield left to begin greeting the Indian leaders, Fargo occupied himself with a careful cleaning of his Colt and the Sharps in the last of the daylight, satisfying himself that they would do their deadly work come the new day. He ate a short meal of jerky and some biscuits taken from the wagon train, then spread his bedroll out under the stars that had risen. He would have preferred to be beyond the limits of the great camp, but it would take some time to walk that far and there was no real point in leaving a place where he would be relatively undisturbed.

As he lay on the bedroll, thoughts churned in his head, of Lucy and her family, of Daisy and her willingness to do whatever it took to sabotage him, of the wholesale slaughter that had been blamed on the Indians for the sake of profit, and of the innocent, if incompetent soldiers who had died defending wagon trains as they crossed the plains. Harry and his men had shown no mercy to those who had crossed their paths. It was clear from the mood in this camp that they would find none tomorrow. He closed his eyes and wrapped sleep around himself.

He had been aware of Amos passing by him and entering the tepee during the night, but when he awoke in the light of the false dawn, Fargo was still surprised to see the wagon master before him. Amos was transformed. He stood naked except for his warrior's paint—red from head to toe, except for a few blue-and-black circles on his chest. Fargo realized that most of the red came from Amos's own blood: he had slashed his arms and was spreading the ruby liquid across his body.

Fargo drew a low breath of surprise.

Amos nodded at him. "Are you ready?"

"I am," Fargo replied. "What more do you have to do?"

"This is it. I am wearing the colors of the sun god."

"Do they think that's who you are?"

"No. But he inspires me to wear his colors."

Fargo brought himself fully awake and saddled the Ovaro. The whole camp was awake and prepared within a few minutes, a legion of angry warriors ready to seek retribution. They set out, Fargo riding with Amos at the front of the swiftly moving army. The Indian scouts reported that Harry had only four men standing watch, and an advance party of braves had already stolen ahead to eliminate the sentries.

The ride to the southwest was grim and silent, a pageant of death-to-come moving in terrible formation. Amos explained that there was no real battle plan. Their tremendous advantage in numbers and the power of surprise over a sleeping camp would make victory fast and sure. For a moment Fargo pitied the men who slept in the camp. But he remembered Lucy's family, and the pity was swept away.

Harry and his men had camped alongside a dry streambed about a half-mile from a rise. If their sentries had been alert, they would have had some notice of the horde riding down upon them. But sharp knives in the early light had dispatched the men who would have given the camp any warning at all. And so it was that the whoops of hundreds of furious braves and the roar of a thousand hooves across the dry plain brought the rumor of death to the ears of Harry's men, who were still sleeping as the war party crested the rise and headed for the camp at full speed.

There was enough time for some of them to leap up and grab their rifles, but as the scouts had said, discipline was lax. Many of the guns were not loaded or near to their owners. The men who were able to rise and fire did some damage, but against the relentless waves of bronzed bodies, they could make little difference.

Fargo lay low across the neck of the Ovaro and charged straight into the center of camp. The slaughter of these marauders would easily be handled by the Indians. He wanted Harry, wanted to capture the man who had planned the destruction and authorized the horrors.

The Ovaro vaulted the bodies of two men, dead with arrows in their chests, and swerved around the end of a wagon. A bullet whizzed by close enough for Fargo to feel its breath upon his cheek, but now he spotted the form of a tall man with dark hair rising up from the back of an Owensboro to fire shots in the direction of a party of Sioux who were setting fire to a wagon full of furniture. With a yell, Fargo dived from the Ovaro's back and into the wagon where the man crouched.

It had to be Harry. The Trailsman grabbed the man by the shoulder and flipped him over, and he could see the cold blue eyes and the lean face. Similar to his, he knew, but far crueler and more devious. Fargo drew back his right fist and was about to bring it down on the man's jaw when pain roared through his groin. He fell back, aching where Harry's knee had caught him.

Harry had grabbed his rifle again and was swinging it around to blow Fargo out of existence. The Trailsman clawed at the Colt in the holster at his side. He tore the gun from its leather harness and got off one shot just as Harry's rifle boomed.

Fargo hadn't had much time to aim, and the slug from the Colt went high. With a *ping!* the bullet ricocheted off the barrel of Harry's gun and disappeared into the slaughter going on around the wagon. The blast from the rifle was thrown high, as well, and if Harry had aimed for Fargo's chest, he might have still killed the man. But he had had his sights on Fargo's head, and the bullet missed putting a permanent crease in the Trailsman's head by about four inches.

There was a brief moment when Fargo wasn't sure if he was still alive. When he realized he was, he could have fired again, but he wanted Harry alive. With a powerful push from his steel-muscled legs, he threw himself into the man. Harry was trying to reload the rifle, but was obviously having a hard time, since Fargo's wild bullet had taken off one of his fingers before it glanced off the rifle barrel.

Harry toppled backward and over the edge of the wagon. Fargo followed, his arms wrapped around the man's waist. Landing on the ground forced the air out of Harry with a whoosh. Once more Fargo pulled up to deliver a hard right to Harry's jaw.

There was a whoop and the briefest impression of a brown blur, and Fargo found himself thrown backward again. He hit his head on the back of the wagon and his mind filled with a rushing darkness that grew and grew as he sagged back and collapsed underneath the Owensboro's bed.

When he awoke, it was to the impression of a bright light overhead and water on his face. Someone was speaking to him, and it took a moment to recognize Amos' voice.

"That's it, keep coming," Amos encouraged.

With a shake of his head that only made him dizzy, Fargo opened his eyes. Obviously the slaughter was over. The air was silent and he and Amos were the only living white men he could see.

"Where's Harry?" Fargo rasped.

Amos shifted to one side, and behind him Fargo could see Harry's body. But not Harry's face. Where his head had been was nothing but a red mass of pulp with a few tufts of black hair.

"I was there"—Amos gestured a few wagons away—"when you got run down. It was one of Harry's horses, loose when his rider got shot. When it ran you down, I figured both of you were dead. But I guess you just got knocked out of the way and banged your head on the wagon."

Fargo sighed, then spat to clear the foul taste out of his mouth. "I wanted him alive. I wanted to know what connection he had to Webster and McCormick."

Amos looked surprised. "He is McCormick. Didn't you know that?"

"No. How the hell should I?"

"I guess you weren't a real regular customer at Lilabeth's. He didn't show up there much. I just figured you knew."

"Well, I didn't," Fargo growled. "Not that it makes much difference." He shoved himself up and to his feet. For a moment the earth seemed to ripple underneath him, but that passed quickly. "Is it done?" he said grimly.

"It is," Amos replied.

"Then it's time for us to go back where we belong," Fargo said. He looked at the big man beside him for a moment, wondering if this taste of blood would pull Amos back to his old way of life.

"Yes, it is," Amos said.

And Fargo knew then that it really was all over.

LOOKING FORWARD!
The following is the opening
section from the next novel in the exciting
Trailsman series from Signet:

**THE TRAILSMAN #93
THE TEXAS TRAIN**

*Texas, 1859, just south of the Concho River,
where the long shadow of the Alamo
still lingered . . .*

The big man's lake-blue eyes peered down at the
flatland below where the train slowly chugged its way
beneath the cloudless, sun-swept sky. There were a
hundred rifle-carrying men riding the four cars, and
alone, all by himself, he was going to attack that train.

Skye Fargo repeated the words again inside himself
as he had done a dozen times over the last hour, as
though he were still trying to make himself believe it.
An oath escaped his lips with the deep breath he took,
and his powerfully muscled shoulders lifted in a half-
shrug. What was he doing here? he asked himself.
How did he let himself get talked into this suicidal,
damn-fool idea? How had he taken leave of his senses?
But then he'd asked himself the same questions for the
past three days as he rode across the Texas country-
side and made ready for this moment.

He had taken a hell of a lot of damn-fool jobs over

the years, but this had to be the granddaddy of them all. But he was here, even though he was still having trouble believing it. The price of hot loins and an active conscience. Either was a terrible burden on a man. Together they were a millstone around his neck. Or was it around something else? The little train continued its slow chugging and Fargo let the days flash backward as he waited.

He'd been in Possum Kingdom, north of Abilene, a hot, bustling little town where he'd finished breaking trail for the Symonds brothers' herd, all the way from the Kansas border. It had been a job too long, too hard, and for too little money, but that was how they turned out sometimes. The Apache had been scarce—he'd been grateful for that—and when it was finished, he'd celebrated with too much bourbon. But that, too, had ended, and he was about to leave Possum Kingdom, watering the magnificent Ovaro at the town trough for the ride back north, when the young woman appeared at his elbow.

He stared at her for a long moment. In Possum Kingdom she was not unlike a starflower in a bog, her beauty startling, unexpected, and misplaced. He took in gray eyes in an even-featured face, high cheekbones, a face of commanding attractiveness under soft brown hair. Her dark-green dress enclosed a slender figure and the square-cut neckline let the tops of beautifully full breasts rise into view.

"Skye Fargo, the Trailsman," she said softly, a statement not a question.

"Bull's-eye," the big man said. "Though I didn't know I was wearing a name tag."

"Riding, not wearing," she said with a smile and a glance at the striking Ovaro still drinking from the trough.

"That all?" Fargo asked, though the horse had been his identity often enough.

"No, I was informed that you were breaking trail

for the Symonds' herd and that you'd end up here," she said, her words uttered with cool, crisp diction. "I must talk to you. I've a room at the inn. Will you go with me, please? It's just down the street."

"Honey, I'd go with you if it was in Mexico," Fargo said. He swung in beside her as she set off down the street.

She walked with a smooth motion that hardly moved her breasts inside the square-necked dress, he noted.

The Possum Kingdom Inn was the most respectable building in town and the only one with a fresh coat of paint on it. Fargo followed the young woman down a ground-floor hallway. She used her room key to open a door and he went in after her, his lake-blue eyes scanning the room at once. One closet, its door open, he saw, the rest of the room ordinary enough, a single bed and a worn dresser with a big white porcelain washbasin on top of it.

The young woman closed the door and turned to him, cool amusement in her gray eyes. "I expect you're curious about this," she said.

"That's the right word, honey," Fargo said. "What's all this about?"

"It's about hiring you," the young woman said.

"You want to hire me?" Fargo questioned with a frown.

"No, not me. I was sent by someone to hire you," she answered.

"Who are you?"

"Jill Foster," she said. "Herbert Standish sent me to hire you for him."

"Who the hell is Herbert Standish?"

"A very wealthy man, a very determined man, a very ruthless man."

"Why didn't he come hire me himself?" Fargo frowned.

"He expected you'd ask that."

"That's one for him. Now, answer the question," Fargo said, a trace of annoyance coming into his voice.

"He thought I'd do a much better job of convincing you to take the job than he would," Jill said.

Fargo half-smiled as his eyes went over the young woman again. "He could be right, there," he remarked. The young woman turned to a small suitcase at the edge of the bed. "What does Herbert Standish want to hire me for?" Fargo asked.

"He wants you to take his daughter off a train," Jill said.

"That doesn't take a trailsman."

"That part will come later," Jill said as she reached into the suitcase and drew out a sheaf of new, crisp bills and put them on top of the dresser in front of him. "There's two thousand dollars there, with two thousand more when you finish the job," she said.

Fargo stared at the money and heard the low whistle that escaped his lips. "That's a lot of convincing money. All to take his daughter off a train?"

"He wants his daughter off that train real bad," Jill Foster said, and Fargo's smile was chiding tolerance.

"I've been around too long. No more sweet talk. What's the catch?"

"There *is* a problem," she said casually. "There will be a hundred armed guards on the train."

Fargo felt his eyebrows arch. "A hundred armed guards?" he echoed. "Yes, I guess you could call that a problem."

"They're soldiers of the Mexican Army," she said, and Fargo knew his brows arched still further. "A hundred soldiers of the Mexican Army up here in Texas?" He frowned. "You've got to be kidding. That'd cause another damn war."

"That's why they'll all be dressed in ordinary clothes. But they're soldiers of the Mexican Army."

"And I'm supposed to go up there all by myself and

172

take the girl," Fargo muttered. "All that money is suicide pay, honey."

"No. Standish is convinced you're the one man who can pull it off. You've a reputation for doing things other men can't do," Jill said.

"I've done a few, but I'm no damn magician."

"It's an awful lot of money to turn down, Fargo," she said with a glance at the sheaf of bills.

"It is, but then I can't spend much of it dead, can I?" the big man answered.

Her shrug was a dismissal of his remark. "Mr. Standish is convinced you won't let that happen."

Fargo appraised Jill Foster and saw her cool, composed manner remained intact, her very attractive face showing only a calm confidence. "Tell me, honey, why doesn't Standish hire his own army of gunhands to attack the train and take the girl?" Fargo asked.

"He figured you'd ask that," Jill said. "He gave me two reasons. First, he'd have no advantage of surprise if he hired a hundred gunhands. Word would get out. Somebody would talk and they'd be ready and waiting on the train. Second, that'd bring on the kind of wild battle that could get the girl killed by any of a thousand stray bullets. He won't risk that."

Fargo turned the answer in his mind and had to agree with Standish's thinking. "He have any ideas on how one man can do what a hundred can't?" he asked with an edge of sarcasm.

"Surprise. Find a way to stop the train. Then find a way to get the girl off. They won't be expecting one man. They'll be looking for an attacking force. He feels one man has the only chance," Jill said.

Fargo turned the answer in his mind and allowed a wry smile. "He could be right, there, but not this man, honey. As a gambling man I knew used to say, I don't like the cards and I don't like the odds. Tell Mr. Standish to keep his money and find a new boy."

"He expected you might say that," Jill answered.

"It's known that money doesn't carry the weight with you that it does with most men."

"True enough, especially where my neck is concerned," Fargo said.

"That's another reason why Mr. Standish sent me to convince you instead of himself," Jill Foster said, her face remaining coolly unsmiling. But her hand went to the top button of the dress, pulled it open, and went down to the next, and Fargo realized his mouth had fallen open as she unbuttoned the entire dress, bent forward gracefully, stepped from it, pulled off bloomers, and turned to face him, gloriously naked. . . .